HARVEST MOON

BY

JOSEPH A. WAILES

OUTLAW PRESS
RAWHIDE, TEXAS

COPYRIGHT © 2014
JOSEPH A. WAILES

ISBN 978-0-9916454-6-6

OUTLAW PRESS
2980 PHYLLIS LANE
RAWHIDE, TEXAS
75234-6425

THE WINNER OF THE HUMAN RACE

BY
JOSEPH A. WAILES

I_WHEN LIGHT BECAME A MAN

II_THE LONGEST NIGHT

III_ANCIENT DREAMS, NEWBORN VISIONS

IV_WAR OF THE BOOK

V_THE THIRD UNIVERSAL EVENT HORIZON

VI_HARVEST MOON

VII_TOO GOOD TO BE UNTRUE

BOOKS AVAILABLE AT OUTLAW PRESS

HARVEST MOON

TABLE OF CONTENTS

0_FOREWORD…………………………....9

1_HARVEST MOON………………..11

2_THE HASHIMITE………………...22

3_TEARS OF COMFORT WOMEN...32

4_THE BIRTH OF THE GREEN HORSE………………………………..42

5_THE POWER OF THE AIR……….63

6_PLOTS WITHIN PLOTS…………..71

7_EXECUTION………………………79

8_THE RIVER OF MERCY OVERFLOWS………………………..97

9_ATTACK OF THE KILLER TORNADOS………………………...104

10_WATER MANAGEMENT……....117

11_THE FIRST TIME I MET GWEN………………………………124

12_WITH ALL DUE RESPECT……126

13_THE LIAR-BREATHING DRAGON…………………………….131

14_FLINT…………………………...143

15_THE GREEN HORSE GALLOPS IN SANDALS..............................149

16_CHICKEN LITTLE WAS RIGHT.....................................155

17_FAITH-BASED CHOCOLATE CAKE..161

18_THE SECOND SPACE RACE...162

19_HEADLESS CHICKENS..........168

20_EARTHQUAKES IN VARIOUS PLACES....................................175

21_WOLVES SENT TO HUNT......179

22_THE HOMETOWN OF EVIL....186

23_OUT THROUGH THE IN DOOR.....................................190

24_ADAM'S FIREPLACE............200

25_CON-MEN IN THREE-PIECE SUITS.....................................214

26_SWARMS WITH STINGERS.....219

27_ONE IS THREE....................228

28_WEAPON OF VALOR.............232

29_THE BEGINNING OF THE END GAME.....................................245

30_SPECIAL OPS.....................254

31_MESSIAH, MESSAGE, MEDIA, MEN.......................................263
32_THE CURSE OF PHAROH.......272
33_THE NEXT TIME I MET GWEN.....................................280
34_IN, FOR THE DURATION.......287
35_ABOUT THE AUTHOR..........299
36_BACK-JACKET TEXT............301

HARVEST MOON

FOREWORD

The writing of these six books has been both the hardest fight, and the greatest joy which my life has so far experienced. The prime goal was to honor our good Lord, and the secondary goal was that the readers would enjoy the books. I have had much positive feedback in regards to these two points. Thank you.

This particular work is launched by the overlapping timelines between end-time Biblical Prophecy, and the events which the nightly, evening network news is currently reporting. It is not intended to offend anyone, but it is the most accurate transcription of the intense dreams granted unto me, and the echoes I see and hear in both Scripture and current events. I hope our good Lord might enable you to also perceive some of the marvels which have flooded my nightly dreams, since I was young.

Forensic scientists use points of congruence to decide whether a face belongs to one person, or another. The more the number of points of intersection, the better is the match.

I see an ever-increasing number of intersection points appearing, and the frequency also appears on the rise. Time is accelerating toward the end. Strap on your helmets.

HARVEST MOON

In ancient times, people would have definitely noticed the event much more. They absolutely would have reacted to it much more strongly. Such a thing would have been far more than just a strange story in the news, or a curious scientific occurrence.

In the second decade of the 21st Century, such a thing was just another blip on the radar, and not really of much interest or significance. At least, that was the way almost everyone on Earth regarded the news.

It happened on the night of 21December2010. That night, a perfect alignment was produced in which the Sun, Earth, and moon all lined up so precisely that a full lunar eclipse appeared. The precise timing of the event, exactly upon the night of winter solstice, was so extremely unusual, that it had not been seen for about four hundred years. Right after the last occurrence, the entire western hemisphere was opened up for settlement, and exploration, and exploitation. In that sequence of historical events, a nation was raised up that would fight to the death, beside Israel, defending the chosen nation from overwhelming enemies.

The time prior to that had signaled the end of the feudal system, and the emergence of modern European nations. In the one before that, the subsequent changes had been the expansion of the Viking people, and their conquest of the entire northern hemisphere, with the exception of the Orient. Even Russia was settled and ruled by Vikings, as were all of the major northern regions of the Earth.

The occurrence prior to that one had just preceded the explosion of the Sumatran super-volcano, Lake Toba. That event had so changed the world climate and weather patterns, that about a third of the world's people starved to death, and all development and growth of northern countries was held back for at least a century, until the micro ice age passed, and that gave the new religion of Islam a chance to become established, and to begin to try to dominate the world. (Mohammed was, reportedly, a demented, demon-possessed, child-abusing sadist, with only the insane drive of an egomaniac, attempting to control the whole world, around himself.)

The winter solstice lunar eclipse before that one had been at the time of the first century church, as martyrs were spilling their blood, to faithfully tell the truth about King Jesus.

The special events, which were to follow the event of 21December2010, were all, at least the major ones, listed in the writings of the Holy Prophets of God, including Revelation. Almost no one in the world realized that the special timing of that Heavenly spectacle was no accident, and that it actually marked the start of the final seven-year endurance run for the saints of King Jesus.

Even though the people in the world did not realize it, the events of world history did know, and they sped along to completion, knowing that they were on a tight schedule. Within a month after that, Tunisia, Egypt, Qatar, Yemen, Syria, Jordan, Iran, and Libya all experienced upheavals. Rulers which had reigned unchallenged for decades, wielding an iron fist, even against their own people, suddenly found themselves fighting to retain power, as the masses of the subjugated victims under their oppression struggled to break those long-worn chains of tyranny. What could be the reason for so widespread and simultaneous a rebellion? The only logical answer is that the good Lord was beginning to clear the path for the rocket-like rise to power of the anti-Christ. After all, the monster had to be firmly in power, controlling the entire world's Muslim population, no later than another three and a half years into the future. Otherwise, the thing could not sign, and then later break, a peace treaty with Israel.

Even if someone had tried to convince the proponents of the so-called "pre-tribulation-rapture" concept that the actual seven year mark had already been crossed, those which were confused by that "pre-tribulation-rapture" notion would reject it for reasons of pride. Such mistaken preachers could never admit that it would actually happen precisely the Way that King Jesus had prophesied that it would, and that no one was going to ever experience a "pre-tribulation-rapture", and the only way out for any Christian, except death, was to stay alive through the entire seven years. After that, yes, the good Lord is going to call all of us up to meet with Him in the air, but that will not be until after the seventh trump, and that is right near the end of the tribulation. Also, the entire Earth will give up all the dead saints in it, even those in the sea, and they will actually arrive first, before any of the REMAINING saints, which are still here, still alive, in their original bodies. So, until the dead are first called up out of their graves, no one is going to get any lucky "escape" out of the tribulation. (Best advice is for people to know and accept the right truth about this, and settle it in their hearts, to just keep following, and obeying, King Jesus, and to found one's personal beliefs upon the Words of King Jesus, and not heed the loudly mistaken believers, which would rather preach a comforting misunderstanding, instead of a troubling truth!) Christianity is not for wimps, or for people looking for an easy way out. King Jesus is the Way, but He is the Way through, not out early! (If you do not think you are committed enough to give your life, and maybe your head, for King Jesus, either become more committed, or give up your pretense at faith.)

Political events were not the only major developments which followed right after the last signal moon. Precisely 90 days later, there appeared a mighty sign in heaven, which is commonly called the "Super Moon". This occurs every 18 years, when the moon is at perigee, and the full moon appears larger then, than at any other time in its' orbit. Eight days prior to the Super Moon, which also marked the start of spring, and the Vernal Equinox, another sign happened upon Earth, namely, a major earthquake, a resultant tidal wave, and a radiation leak that is so far unequaled in world history. Another troubling phenomenon is the widespread drought, which currently affects large parts of North America, Russia, Australia, China, Africa, and the Middle East. Oil prices are rising again, rapidly, aggravated by all the uproar in the Middle East. Solar activity is on the increase, and many large solar flares are presenting, with increased intensity, and frequency. This all occurred within six months of the massive and deadly oil spill into the Gulf of Mexico.

When the people of Earth begin to see signs in Heaven, upon Earth, and, in the nations of the world, massive changes and rebellions, then perhaps the people of the Earth should begin to fall to their knees, and start praying, right now!

It does make a real difference unto which god you do pray, since there is only One God. If a person is not praying to Him Who is Father, Savior, and Holy Spirit, then the person is an idolater, and a devil-worshipper, by definition of terms. One can either worship the real God, or prepare to be thrown into the Lake of Fire. It seems like a simple choice, unto a believer, but unless one is reborn, of the Holy Spirit, a person cannot believe, or trust the real God. (Unbelievers should be pitied, and witnessed unto, and prayed for, but should not be feared, or despised.)

The seven years of conflict will strip all of the masks of pretense and deception off of the Muslims, and their lies, just as the recent burning of a copy of the Koran triggered a wave of hatred and murder, all across Afghanistan, despite years of investment in money and lives, by Americans trying to bring peace to a violent gathering of madmen. Also, there is now no more pretending at good will between the Arabians and the Americans, since the ruling desert bandits of Arabia did not like the removal of Mubarak from Egypt. Now, they fear for their own skins.

So, at the very least, the stresses and conflicts of the years ahead, until sometime in 2017, 2018, or thereabouts, will boil away all lies, all liars, and all people that are not serious, as in, life-and-death serious, about their commitment to King Jesus. To separate wheat from chaff, one must hurl the wheat and chaff together into the air, and the power of the wind will drive away the chaff, leaving only the wheat. So it will be at the end of this age, when the wind of the Holy Spirit will drive away the chaff off of the Earth, and only the wheat will remain behind, with the good Lord. What we are seeing, now, is the beginning of the "hurling into the air" phase.

So, yes, please, I would choose to be "left behind", along with all the sincere, honest, humble Christians, and not blown away with the liars of the world. I do not wish to be gathered into a bundle, to be thrown into the Lake of Fire. (Neither would I want to be found to be a Christian, but one that told a false prophecy about our good King Jesus!) King Jesus came here once, from Heaven, to save us. He will do so again, when the moment is right, just as He said.

Before that happens, the Sun will not shine, and the moon will not give forth its' light, before that great and notable Day of the Lord! (In a very literal sense that precise moment did indeed occur, on the night of 21December2010. Those of us who did witness the eclipse that strange night did not see the light of the Sun, and the moon did not give forth its' light, either, for about an hour!)

Remember, how an angel said, in Revelation, unto King Jesus, "Thrust in Thy sickle, and reap: for the time is come for Thee to reap; for the harvest of the Earth is ripe!"

21December2010 was the final Harvest Moon. Seek King Jesus, now, or be blown away, soon. Prepare now for harvest!

THE HASHIMITE

He looked out at the sunset, from his viewpoint, several hundred feet up over the city. It was a deep red splash of sky, with orange, fiery thunder clouds further west, forming over Israel. The sun blazed into and through the gaps within the storm system, as it blew in from the Mediterranean, driven by a spring squall.

His eyes turned, as always, toward the south, where usurpers had stolen, and occupied, his family's lands, for nearly seventy years. Instead of being just another non-descript middle-eastern oil king, with one of the smallest countries, and almost no military, he should have been ruling the biggest country, with the most oil, and the greatest wealth. His father had just accepted the outrage, being absolutely powerless to overturn it. The son was not a man to overlook such a thing, even decades later.

The recent events in nearby countries, and his own, had forced his plans into action much sooner than he would have liked. Since the trials of Mubarak, and his sons, had just begun, it would only be a few weeks now, before he had to have his main pieces in place, and be ready to move.

The first move had already been made, last week, even before the trials had actually started. He wanted to be the first one to make an offer to the Egyptians. Other kings would also see the advantage, but not until after he had made his deal with them. The Arabians, his arch enemies, and the afore-mentioned robbers of his family's lands, had been giving a lot of grief to Obama, ever since they sort of forced Mubarak out. The Arabians had a long standing deal with both the U.S., and also the Egyptians, and a lot of under the table money was exchanged, on all sides. When Mubarak was lost, a lot of that system broke down, and the Arabians lost a lot of hidden money. They were warning the U.S. not to encourage any such thing in Arabia, or else. ("Or else", what? Why, cut off Arabian oil, of course!)

Abdullah was the sort of king that kept well-informed, and knew of all the other uprisings, and so forth, all over the region. It always was a reminder to him, deliberately done, when his father, King Hussein, had named him for their arch enemy, King Abdullah of Arabia. It was an oath the son had sworn, to avenge their family's dishonor, no matter how long he had to wait, to achieve it.

He knew that Pakistan had also been saber-rattling at the U.S., since their Predators had killed a lot of innocent Pakistanis. The U.S. would soon be sending yet more troops to Afghanistan and Pakistan, to avoid a total loss there, and that would stretch the U.S. military presence pretty thin. As the U.S. did operations in the tribal areas, they were slowly winning the military aspect of the conflict, and steadily recruiting more young militants for the opposition.

It was a calculated risk, but his friend in Egypt was the secret high commander of the Egyptian military, and would likely soon become the next modern Pharaoh. Syria was in upheaval, and Assad was not a team player, anyway. He was way too busy, butchering his own revolutionaries, to be a part of it. With the Egyptian military and the vastly smaller, but still effective, in small scale, Jordanian military combined, a lightning night strike against Arabia would destroy its' airpower, overwhelm its' defenses, and leave the sand open for Jordanian tanks to roll in, and occupy Riyadh.

Of course, the protestors left behind would not hesitate to start more trouble, if most of the army suddenly stormed south. He would give orders to enforce martial law, before he left, and protestors would be killed. The oil kings did not care a thing about free speech, or human rights. Such things seemed alien to their culture.

Now he needed to get his friends in Pakistan to launch assaults against U.S. troops there, once the Egyptians were ready to roll. That would draw off some U.S. strength, so the Egyptians and Jordanians could take Arabia, thus restoring his family's honor, and giving control of most of the world's oil to just three countries. From there, they would slam into Baghdad, drowning the Iraqi military like ants in a flood, since the U.S. was already greatly vacated from Iraq, and more troops were leaving every day. The strength of Iraq in the old days would have prevented this, but the U.S. had broken them, and what was there now was no match for a real invasion. These two moves had to be done back to back, since the Turks would be looking with hungry eyes toward Baghdad, unless he got there first, and claimed it.

Once those two nations fell, his Pakistani friends would sweep west across Afghanistan, with their entire army, and give an ultimatum to Iran, like fight for us, or die. The Iranians were still working on building a nuke, but the Pakistanis had already had them, for ten years. They knew how to use them, too, and India knew it, so they would not ever invade Pakistan, as long as 100 Pakistani soldiers still could launch nuke missiles toward India. The Indians knew the Pakistanis were crazy enough to do it, too.

While all that happened, a small section of the vast Egyptian military would head due west, helping the rebels in Libya, and removing Gaddafi. The psycho was too insane to trust in any alliance. That would give them pretty much the entire oil production belt throughout the whole middle east, and would therefore give them the greatest economic and military control possible, not just of that region, but of the whole world's economy.

This whole thing had started at the end of World War II, when white Europeans had carved up the Middle East, to suit their own agendas. Churchill might be a hero to the British, but the Hashimite hated him forever. He was the one who had forcibly removed his family from Mecca, and Medina, after centuries of living there. Their blood line ran straight back to Mohammed. The Hashimites were his blood line heirs, and were charged with the keeping of the Arabian land, especially Mecca and Medina. To take it away, and give it to some Bedouin camel riders, was just about as degrading a thing as they could do to the heirs of Mohammed!

So, even though it would take a few years, maybe three or four, all of the Muslim nations in the world would follow him, once they began to believe that he was their Mahdi. Sooner or later, every nation upon Earth would trade with him, or tremble and die before him. In mockery of the World War II agreement, which had been forced upon them, he would make a treaty with Israel, and give Israel back the West Bank, the Temple Mount, the Gaza strip, and everything else they wanted, and move the Palestinians back to where they originally came from, which was the country where he was standing, right now, this evening. That would thrill the Palestinians, and the Hebrews, and such a treaty would lull the whole world into thinking that he was a reasonable guy, who only sought world peace. Soon, the whole world would idolize him. Literally.

Ultimately, he could exert such a ferocious stranglehold upon the entire world, that he would make them all, every person, give him a cut of every sale. In fact, he would not let them buy or sell, unless they registered every single transaction, great or small. They would have to have microchips implanted under their skin, so he could keep track of all of them, even by satellite. Those who tried to disobey would be publicly beheaded.

He would set up his new capital in Baghdad, and rename it Babylon. After all, that was what the entire country had been called, back in 600 B.C.

Once he got everything established there, and had the whole world system in place, he would mobilize the armies of the world into a united, focused push against Israel. There was one oath which he valued even more than the one, of which his own name reminded him, constantly. Every Hashimite son, in the long generations since their ancestor Mohammed, had had to swear, upon his 12th birthday, to never forget the blood oath between his family, and the sons of Israel. As the direct line descendant of the original Mohammed, this was a special duty, and the purpose for the entire religion of Islam. It was why Mohammed had started Islam in the first place. It was a hatred which spanned centuries, and covered the whole world. As large as the whole world was, it was always going to be way too small for the sons of Israel, and the sons of Mohammed, to ever find room enough for peace. One side had to die, or the other would.

As a western-educated man, the fellow had even read a fair amount of the Bible, but regarded it as Western fables. His eyes were always blinded by hatred, and his heart was always hardened by pride.

King Jesus would have saved him, but he never would listen to Him. Abdullah always thought that he should become the king of the world, never realizing that King Jesus Christ already is King of Everything!

TEARS OF COMFORT WOMEN, AND SILENT SCREAMS OF FINLESS SHARKS

Almighty God looked down upon a certain nation, and watched the people there for a long time, for well over a century. He understood that their attitude was in part because their very much larger and far more powerful next door neighbor nation had cruelly oppressed them in centuries gone by. This nation, an island nation, had become utterly ruthless and cold hearted, whenever they dealt with any other people, or even the other creatures of the Earth, and seas. They were driven by raw pride, and absolute self-centered evil, and had lived only to try to dominate the whole rest of the world under their boots.

About a century earlier, this nation had enslaved a nation to the north, another island nation, one that was smaller and weaker, at the time of the conflict. The victor had immediately taken their choices of the women of the victims, and shipped them off to the south, to serve out the rest of their lives as forced sex-slaves, serving the lusts of the conquering army's soldiers, while being held for decades in prison camps. Those women were called "comfort women". These prison camps also were the scenes of the forced rapes, which numbered in the hundreds of thousands, and continued, unabated, for thirty five hellish years, until the perverts were crushed by a mighty champion of a nation, from across the sea. Then, the women were liberated, and the practice was forever stopped.

During the World War II, this nation had been one of the first, and worst, aggressors, launching many unprovoked attacks against other people and cultures.

They fought very dirty, torturing their victims to death, delighting in the screams of misery and horror. They had spread their devil-worshipping evil all over the whole Pacific Ocean, and all of Asia, and were barely stopped from invading the Americas. They were so crazy with manic pride, that in the end, only actual nuclear war was capable of making them surrender, or die. It was the first case in which nuclear weapons had to be used in warfare.

After the end of the war, the nation slowly entered back into the world arena, through trade, and learned how to slice into transistors and integrated circuits, one very thin layer at a time, making a photographic record of the internal circuits there, and then patent-jumping the circuits, until they learned enough to develop some innovations of their own, and then to snag a huge share of the world's consumer electronics market, and also a lot of the world's auto market. (The world later found out that cheaper does not usually mean better!) Their metallurgy science did grow by leaps and bounds, since they only had second-hand steel to use, not fresh ore.

The nation used the new economic clout to wage a type of economic struggle, in which the moves were more like a chess game, for very high stakes, with a dash of poker, and some Russian roulette thrown in as well. Markets grew, and died, and new ones were born, but the game continued.

One of the nation's greatest sources of income came from the ocean. Fish was the specialty of these folks, and had always been, since the land did not support enough agriculture to feed all of the population there. In recent years, eating the strange raw fish "delicacies" of these people had become a world-wide fashion statement of the very snooty snobs of the restaurant scene. Even special restaurants, dedicated to just that sort of raw fish diet, showed up everywhere, even in Oklahoma, and Nebraska!

The problem was not that the good Lord minded anyone having fish for dinner. Of course not! He, Himself, had often enjoyed a fish or two with His disciples, when He walked among us. No, that was not the trouble.

The thing that really bothered Him a lot was that the particular people did not usually kill the fish, before they started to eat it. Even if they did, they did cruelly, without any humane regard for the suffering or the agony of the creature that they were murdering. Skinning a fish, or any other creature, while it still lives, is insanely cruel, and cannot be justified by saying anything about "keeping it fresh!"

The final straw was when the good Lord looked down and saw that the fishermen had become so evil and heartless, that when they caught a shark, (which was prized for the much-coveted shark fins, which were considered a special, expensive delicacy) they instantly cut off the fins, and then heartlessly dumped the still living, now crippled (and suffering, in absolute agony!) helpless creature back overboard, to sink and drown, dying in hopeless pain and darkness.

After He saw that, something snapped inside His calmness, and deep in the heart of the most patient Person that ever lived, rage stirred against those sub-human, two-legged animals, and He moved.

With one mighty fingertip, He reached down into the world, and thrust His great hand deep into the sea, and with one light touch against the floor of the ocean, produced a monumental, historically huge earthquake, which knocked down buildings all over the island nation. That was just for openers.

As He withdrew His mighty hand, the unseen shockwave was already racing outwards, in all directions, and in many forms. The primary shock traveled through the ground, and was measured all over the Earth. The secondary shock was induced by that primary shock, and traveled through the water.

While it was out in open water, it only appeared to be about three or four feet tall. Yes, that was what it was, in the open ocean. The only problem came when the high speed wave reached the shallow area near shore, where its' massive momentum, and its' unimaginable weight, mounted it up on top of itself, and it became a racing mountain of water, maybe thirty, forty, or a hundred feet tall! (Trying to outrun the monster was impossible, unless one could run at eighty miles an hour, or so.) As with the iceberg, most of the racing monster wave traveled under the surface. (At least, until it was ready to strike!)

The wave slammed into some of the most offensive fishing cities, which ranged all up and down the coast. Many people died, and many of them were good people, but many were very bad, indeed. The good Lord had all of the needed angels standing by, to dispatch each person to the appropriate destination, as their time came. Some were spared, but many were not. One thing that was destroyed was the largest part of the group of fishermen which fished for the sharks. For a while, at least, the poor sharks could live in the sea, as God had intended for them, without being heartlessly mutilated and murdered for profit.

Almighty God looked down upon the nation, and pointed at them with His mighty hand, still dripping seawater, and then growled a stern rebuke at them, as His noble Face was still tight with anger.

"I warned you to repent of your heartless ways, and to show love, and kindness, unto each other, and unto My other creatures. My friends the Americans delivered the message for Me, if you will recall the two very bright, hot flashes that your fathers and grandfathers saw, years ago. I gave you much time to repent, and to grow the heart of a man, instead of your hearts of stone. You still will not hear Me, but you want to worship your ancestors, and your own pride, instead. Okay, see if they can save you, then. I have heard the tears of the "comfort women", and their families left behind to mourn them, and their torment. I have heard the silent screams of the dying sharks. I saw all of the horrors which you have forced upon those weaker than yourselves, always destroying every one else's lives around you."

"Now, because you still stiffen your necks, and pray to your powerless, dead ancestors, instead of hearing and obeying Me, and learning to show goodness and mercy, I will also send upon you a plague of ruin, with radiation, and economic disaster, and disease, and shame. You will become disgraced before the whole world, since you have acted disgracefully against the world, and the whole Earth, and its' living creatures. Did you not know that I made them as well as you, and I love all of them, too?"

"This is your very last warning! Repent, and be kind, and humble, and give up your vain ways, now! Do this, and live. Disregard, and see what happens next!"

THE BIRTH OF THE GREEN HORSE

They had all arrived by various means of travel, all carefully pre-arranged. Some came by planes, some by trains, a couple by cars, and some even arrived riding horses. The gathering had been called in January, but it had taken until April to assemble all the participants.

What had sparked the sudden ignition of action was a simple thing. A radical Baptist preacher in the U.S. had burned a copy of the Koran. It might seem trivial, and, indeed, in the greater scheme of things, it truly was miniscule, but the radical Jihad maniacs used it as a rallying cry against Israel, and their buddies, the "Crusaders". (You know: the U.S., Britain, and anyone else that stood up for Israel.)

That was the official line. It amazed the West to see how fast the "good-will" and "rapport" carefully sought over the last decade, in Afghanistan, had evaporated in a few hours, and the locals all went berserk, killing many U.N. workers, while still taking millions every month from the U.S. taxpayers, to subsidize their poppy fields. The part that was the most offensive was that the U.S. had paid much more dearly in American lives, even with all the billions wasted there, trying to make idiots act wisely. All of that was for nothing, if the burning of a single copy, of a single book, could incite madmen to commit mass murder. (It was deep in their evil hearts, the whole time.)

The actual reason was one that slipped right by the attention of most of the people upon Earth. The spies, and the spy techniques, of the radicals, were improving. They knew long before the U.S. launched a brand new, top secret military satellite, in early April, 2011. They only could guess what it could, and might, do to their plans for world domination. It was a sudden unknown variable, which threw off all of their calculations, and made victory far less certain.

They knew enough about U.S. satellite and weapons technology to fear them, and so, action had to begin, almost immediately, before the U.S. could launch more of the invisible killer satellites.

That was what had prompted the call to assembly. The hue and cry about the book-burning was just a simple slogan to keep the less intelligent among the followers in line, and fired up to seek to shed Western, and Hebrew, blood. So, while the West celebrated Easter, and Israel celebrated Passover, the major players from the Arabic speaking cultures had been assembled, to form a new, massive block of nations, to move against their enemies.

Once the nine invited guests had arrived in Peshawar, they were moved in black limousines to a small private airport, and driven into a hangar, and out the back side of the hangar, into the dark area behind the hangar, where two large, black helicopters waited, engines already running. They were led onto the larger of the birds, and they both lifted off, extremely quietly, unlike what one usually expected from large helicopters.

These were special, ultra-secret Russian helicopters. They each had two five-bladed rotor assemblies, stacked one on top of the other, and both rotor assemblies ran at the same time, and the same speed, but in opposite directions. This design cancelled out the need for a tail rotor, and added superior stability, and vastly increased lift, so that the jet turbine engines could be fitted with extreme mufflers, without too much loss to power. Thus, the ultra smooth, strong, very quiet helicopters worked perfectly.

They were of stealth material and design. The Russians had been learning new tricks from watching their American competitors. The five blades reduced the air-thumping noise by more than half, and the slower speed of the dual rotors also kept noise down.

The one in which the delegates were riding was a transport, but it had a lot of tough weapons on it, too.

The escort was strictly a hunter-killer. It was very deadly. Twenty Apaches and a dozen fighter jets might be able to take it out, but not much less than that. As far as the U.S. satellites were concerned, these things were both invisible. They were also the most expensive aircraft ever built, except for the Space Shuttle. They were unique, since these were the precious prototypes, and, if lost, would be irreplaceable, at least for another year. That alone indicated just how important the Russians thought that this conference was.

The helicopters sped westward into Afghanistan, threading at hundreds of miles per hour through the mountains, following the contours of the terrain, but at extreme speed, almost matching a jet. These craft had enough fuel to go a long way, at high speed, and the transport even had extra fuel for both of them, if needed.

They flew without lights, and the snow draped peaks reflected enough moonlight to see the sheer walls racing close by the choppers, on each side. The hunter led the way, flying by infrared, and the transport kept pace right behind.

Just before daylight, they cleared the mountains, and turned north, deeper into the province of North Waziristan. After a little while, they suddenly turned back toward a tall cliff, the side of one of the outermost peaks. They sped at high speed straight toward the side of the mountain, and all the passengers were shouting to stop, and turn, and crying out to their moon god, about how great he was, if he would only save them from death!

Suddenly, they could see a hidden crevice, wide enough, barely, to fly into, which they did! After a couple of hundred yards, the crevice opened up a bit more, and then the whole channel canyon took a hard left turn, which the choppers made easily, since they had reduced speed steadily, once they entered the canyon. Suddenly ahead was a sealed overhang, and then they flew under its' huge rock roof, which completely concealed everything inside the box-canyon, for a space of about a quarter mile. The pilots lit their blazing searchlights, and everyone could clearly see the whole canyon. The effect was like a gigantic, vaulted-roof cave, a quarter mile long, four hundred feet tall, and about a hundred feet wide. The floor area was surprisingly level, and the choppers set down, quietly, raising a bunch of dust in the night, which was brilliantly lit, here inside the "cave", both by a lot of artificial light, from many fluorescent fixtures all over the walls of the little canyon, which had been automatically lit, and, also, the dazzling lights from the choppers, which showed everyone the full size and extent of the canyon, but left them all blinking. The pilots shut off the engines, and the passengers followed their Russian escorts into a deeper cave, leading into the wall of the canyon. The pilots began re-fueling both birds for the return flight.

Within a hundred feet into the cliff wall, the cave passage opened up much wider, and more artificial lights revealed a smooth path into a large open cave, where an area about eighty feet across was opened unto them.

There was some furniture at the far wall. A large conference table, several couches, recliner chairs, flat screen televisions, computers, a versatile, high tech kitchen area, and a lot of rifles and machine guns in racks, along the wall, were some of the things that the visitors saw.

What locked their attention were the people already seated at the conference table. A few of the less composed among them actually stumbled, a step or two, and gasped, when they saw the faces of the men which were seated there.

Some of them were obvious, as likely candidates, among the arriving visitors. Abdullah of Jordan, along with Ahmadinejad, of Iran, and the shadowy general of the Egyptian army, which was the close secret partner of Abdullah, although none of the famous ones even knew his name, yet, and a representative of the Libyan revolutionary army, and a representative from the Syrian underground resistance, and a representative from the Palestinians, which were still actually the ancient Edomites, and a man from Yemen, and the most powerful Pashtun warlord, who could command and force all of the tribes in Afghanistan to follow him into battle, and the man that was most likely to become the next strong ruler of Iraq, after the U.S. finished leaving, were the folks that walked into the cave.

The men at the table were Musharraf, of Pakistan, two unknown men in military desert camouflage, with trim, but complete beards, and short hair, (men who stared with ice-cold, dead blue eyes at everyone, and somehow made a person shiver, deep in their bone marrow, just with that stare) and a person none of them ever thought that they would actually see in the flesh. Most of them thought that he had already been dead for years.

The ghost seated there was Osama Bin Laden. He also stared at everyone with icy eyes, but his weathered features at least still sported the trace of a deceitful smile at the corners of his wide mouth.

The guides seated the men at specific places, leaving the head of the table deliberately empty. The two military strangers were each at the first spots next to the head chair, and next to one of them was Musharraf, and next to the other one was Bin Laden. The table was not a strict rectangle, but more of a large oval. This design still designated a head spot, but made around the table visibility much better, for those intense eye-to-eye battles.

As soon as the guides had everyone seated, and water glasses and pitchers were set down, one of the military men spoke, with a strong Russian accent, but in perfect Arabic. He said, "Most of you already know each other, or at least you know the identity of everyone else, except perhaps our Pashtun friend, and I will make sure he is clear on everything later. My partner and I are here from Chechnya, and we are both special ops veterans, and we have been sent by the

KGB, to help fit the pieces of this strange puzzle together. Do not be alarmed, we are just as Muslim as you are!"

He paused a few moments, to let that weighty news sink in, and then continued, "What we are after is all of the oil in the world. The most effective way obtain that is to capture, or convince, the entire Middle East to trade with Russia, and not the U.S. Without enough oil, the U.S. will die. The problem is that the same is true for Russia."

The spy went on, "You may have noticed that there are some oil kings that were not invited to this event, to found a new confederacy of oil kings. Gaddafi and Assad are both loose cannons, and soon either their own people will kill them, or else, we will. We are already placing hit squads in both cases, and also we have already contacted men which will work with us, once we place them in positions of control."

"The U.S. did not please their temperamental buddies, the Arabian Bedouins, in the matter of Mubarak. Soon, there will be so much world-wide conflict, at so many places, that in time, the U.S. will no longer be able to play world-cop, and will have stretched their military, and their military budget, to the snapping point. Arabia will be ripe for the taking!"

"The problem is not a simple knot to untangle, however. We have plans already about Arabia, and Libya, and Syria, but there is still another country, which has been a problem, for a long time. Turkey is very stubborn, and always plays both ends against the middle. Yes, they are technically a part of NATO, but, they will sellout the West in a heartbeat, if they see any advantage for themselves. Until now, we have dealt with them only in unofficial manners, with untraceable deals and trade-offs. Why they are a significant concern now, is that they also know that the U.S. has almost performed all that it will do in Iraq, and the Turks see a huge possibility of invasion and conquest, which would give them a geographical advantage, and a huge increase of their oil stocks."

"We could just let them take it, and then go in right after that, and kill the Turks, but that would likely cause much damage to the oil production capacity of Iraq, and maybe even a larger area. The smarter strategy is to pre-empt their move, and then intensely fortify our position in Iraq."

At this point, the man from Iraq could sit still no longer, and he stood up from the table, and shouted, "Okay, so where does that leave us, the Iraqis?"

The Russian smiled, and calmly answered, "Why, it leaves you in charge, of all the oil resources in Iraq, just as long as you sell it to us, and not to the West!" The Russian's facial expression, along with his deep, steady voice, sent chills deep into the hearts of everyone there, except Bin Laden. He thought that the Russians wanted to keep him alive, to use as a figurehead for the movement.

The man from Iraq visibly calmed himself, with a couple of deep breaths, and sat quietly back down.

The Russian continued, "So, we need a way to forcibly convert or capture these regions: Libya, Syria, Arabia, and Turkey. We are already in progress in Libya, Syria, and Turkey. Arabia we will handle another way."

He went on, "Even though all of you are Muslims, you may not all be aware that we have here among us a very special, honored guest."

When he said that, everyone's eyes landed upon Bin Laden, but the Russian said, "No, Osama is not the one to whom I refer. Although he is very popular in the Arab cultures, his personal fame and legend are useful mostly for inspiring and motivating the ignorant foot soldiers of Islam."

"The one to whom I allude is a direct, actual blood-line descendant of Mohammed, all the way down through time, since the sixth century, from Mecca and Medina. He knows who he is, and now, you all will, too. Will the rightful king of Islam please stand and take his proper place, at the head of our table?"

As he said that, a few of them shifted nervously in their chairs, uncertain what to do. One or two of them almost stood up to walk to the head of the table, and they each re-considered it. Suddenly, and with no fanfare, Abdullah of Jordan stood quietly up, walked calmly over to the head of the table, pulled out the chair, and sat down, silently staring a deadly challenge into each of their puzzled eyes. No one spoke for a while.

After a couple of minutes, the Russian spoke again, and said, "Welcome, o king! Now, all of us will swear an oath of life-

and-death loyalty unto you, or the one who refuses will die, now."

As soon as he said this, the Pashtun chief stood up, with a shout, and said, "Never! The Pashtun are free, and will never bow to anyone!"

Even as he had stood, another silent figure had instantly moved over to him, and a sword whished through the air, and Ahmadinejad smiled grimly, as the Pashtun's head fell to the floor, and his body dropped, still twitching, to begin spilling a large pool of blood upon the cave floor. The Iranian wiped his sword with the robe of his victim, and sheathed it again, then quietly returned to his seat.

As he saw this, Abdullah, their new king, smiled and said, "Okay, I guess the man from Iran is willing to fight and kill for our side!"

Ahmadinejad nodded slightly, and then said, "Either that, or die myself!"

Everyone laughed, very nervously.

Nothing makes a man's plans uncertain

near as much as suddenly learning that there are now new rules, to this deadly contest, and the price of failure is death.

Abdullah spoke again, saying, "That was indeed appropriate, since Afghanistan was part of the Persian Empire, and, we will honor the ancient obligations and responsibilities that were founded centuries ago. Since you are going to be the ruler of modern Persia, yes, you must keep your own region obedient to us. The rest of you will each follow that example. Is there any disagreement?"

Everyone, including the Russians, mumbled answers like, "No, sir!" and, "Of course not!" That made Abdullah smile. He turned to the Russian at his right hand, and said, "Please continue with our strategy session."

The Russian nodded, and said, "So, we must take Arabia, but not yet, not until the West is already too tied up in things in Europe and Asia, to be effective in protecting the Bedouins. Instead, we will begin to drive a hard wedge between Arabia, and the U.S., and also another wedge between Turkey, and the rest of NATO. If Turkey joins us, well. If not, we will make an example out of them, and no other country will try to resist us. After that, we will take Arabia, too, and horribly kill all the members of the so-called "royal household". Following that, any country foolish enough to fight back will be broken, with all our weapons."

As he paused for a breath, Abdullah asked, "Is the Russian military committed to help us, even with nuclear weapons?"

The two Russians locked eyes across the table, and then the second one spoke, for the first time. "We must get final approval from Putin, but he has already told us that that would be okay, if he deems it necessary, to achieve our objectives. He said that he would retain the final veto about that, since, after all, the weapons belong to the Russians!"

Abdullah barked a sharp laugh, without humor, and said, "Well, tell him to make his mind up now, that if he wants to buy or trade oil from us, he better get on board, and stay that way. After all, the oil belongs to the Muslims!"

"Also, tell him not to be absent from the next conference, next month, right here, again. I want him personally in on our planning sessions, to avoid confusion, or contention. As you may realize, I will run a tight ship, in these things."

Meanwhile, in a small village in Afghanistan, a little girl rolled over, and fell back asleep, ignoring the wet tears that stained her pillow. As she drifted off, she began to see a dream/vision of a Hebrew Man, and beside Him, a bright, strong angel. The Man spoke to her, and said, "Rest well, now, little one. The animal that took away your mother, and killed your father and your brothers, has been ejected from his own worthless life, now. He will never hurt you, or anyone else, never again. One day, I will show you just what I am doing to punish him. I will leave one of My angels here with you. From now on, peace will be given unto you. Change is on the Way!"

POWER OF THE AIR?

Adam and Eve stood watching the disaster unfold. Beside them stood Wolf and She-wolf, growling with anger, as all of them were forced to watch, forbidden to intervene or help.

They actually saw the enemy stir up the wind, and force it into a tight spin, and intensify the strength, as it hurtled toward Tuscaloosa. The cherub Michael was already approaching the devil, streaking like a missile right at him!

Just as the funnel cloud, a solid wedge over a mile and a half wide, with winds of almost 300 miles per hour, slammed into the edge of Pleasant Grove, Alabama, Michael slammed into the devil, hitting him with a force far in excess of the huge storm that was killing Christians upon Earth. The devil was knocked back, hitting the ground hard, and trying desperately to squirm out from under Michael, as the stronger cherub began to violently beat and attack the devil.

Michael had arrived just in the very split-second knick of time, since, if he had landed any later, all of northern Alabama, including Birmingham, Tuscaloosa, and every single human life contained within them would have been flattened, exploded, or vacuumed up into the sky, to disappear forever. The storm was running along on its' own momentum, now, and would eventually wind down, but it was no longer receiving strength from the devil. The devil was just struggling to escape from the murderous rage of Michael.

As they rolled around upon the Earth, locked in death grips with each other, Michael had his mighty hand around the devil's throat, and was choking him so hard that the devil had to struggle to get any words out at all. Still, with maximum effort, it managed to croak out, "Mercy!"

At the sound of that, Michael roared a huge laugh, right in the devil's face, and said, in a very intense whisper, "Okay, I will give you just as much mercy as you gave King Jesus!" He began to finish collapsing the devil's windpipe, smiling grimly as he squeezed tighter still.

Suddenly, they both heard the voice of King Jesus, as He told Michael, "Not yet, friend! Save the final death for his time in the fire!"

Michael did not yet loosen his deadly grip, but softly said, "As You command, my Lord, but are You sure we cannot just go ahead and silence this filthy liar, once and for all?"

In reply, they heard King Jesus laugh a delighted laugh, and say, "Not just yet. His lies I will overthrow, from now on, but I want him to pay the full price which I have already assigned to him, and that will take him a very long time in the Fire! For now, just throw him out of there."

Instantly obedient, Michael immediately threw the devil by the neck out into space, far out beyond the moon, and then turned his attention to forcibly slowing down the huge tornado. He began to grab and hold tight onto the strands of the winds, and held them tighter and tighter, until the thing began to break apart into many smaller, but much less deadly, storms. Even as quickly as he worked, the thing still did a very mean job upon Tuscaloosa, but many good angels were already down there among the people, fighting all of the hell-demons, lifting a person clear here, shielding a person there, catching a puppy dog or a kitten as it flew through the air, and setting them down gently. There were thousands of good angels, some fighting and driving away the demons, and some acting out mighty acts of rescue and shelter, as the storm was beginning to die off.

The great cherub Gabriel stood beside Adam and Eve, scowling down in anger, also. Wolf had looked up at him, as if to ask, "Why don't you go help Michael beat the devil up?"

Gabriel noticed, and smiled grimly, and answered, "He does not need my help, Wolf, not right now. Any one of us, the three good cherubs, can whip the devil one-on-one, any time, any place. He was always the weakest of the four of us, and, since he has become the dragon, he is even weaker than he originally used to be. That was one of the things that made him turn bitter, since he blamed King Jesus for making him the weakest. The other thing that got to him was the notion that any creatures with a dirt body could ever be considered nobler than him, and be given the honor of becoming the children of Light, since none of the angels, and none of the cherubs, was ever going to have that gift."

As Gabriel was speaking, King Jesus suddenly appeared there, standing beside them, and they all bowed heads before Him, but He told them, "Yes, friends, watch now, and see what good I will bring out of this mess. Many lives have been lost, and much suffering has begun, but the people of Alabama still love Me, and the world will now see that to be the proven truth, as they praise Me anyway, and help each other to rebuild their shattered lives and homes. I will also send them very much help from all over the nation, and at last, the shame of the good people of Alabama will be forgotten."

"No longer will folks think of Alabama as a place of intense racial hatred, and a people divided. Selma and Birmingham will come to mean new, better things in the months ahead, and the wounds of the past will begin to heal. The storm did not discriminate, but killed whites and blacks alike, since the devil just wants to kill everyone anyway."

"It does irritate Me, though, that the insurance companies and politicians always call a tornado an 'act of God!' If I want to act to destroy anyone, I will use earthquakes, tidal waves, comets, meteors, hailstones as heavy as a hundred pounds, lightning, and so forth. The enemy was initially assigned the power of the air, but he has misused it ever since the Garden. If people would read the testimony of My servant Job, they would begin to understand that it is the devil that destroys their lives, not Me!"

They all stood with King Jesus, watching silently, and then Adam mused aloud, "Is it not true that the devil owns the politicians and the insurance companies, anyway?"

King Jesus turned and smiled at him, and answered, "Yes, for now, but that will be ending, before much longer! Watch, and see, in this next week, while I take away one of the devil's favorite madman servants, and send real terror all through the ranks of the devil's followers. As the enemy has attacked My friend, the U.S., which stands with Israel, I will give honor unto the U.S., and work destruction against their enemies! I will break one of the serpent's fangs!"

PLOTS WITHIN PLOTS

The transport chopper lifted off quietly, and smoothly, carrying all of the members of the new alliance back to Peshawar, where they would catch their own planes home to their own countries.

It was just after total darkness had settled in at the strange little box canyon/hideout that the chopper left. The meeting had lasted all day long, as many details were hammered out. One thing they all had agreed upon was that Abdullah of Jordan, the son of the old King Hussein of Jordan, was now their official leader. To rebel meant certain death, from the more radical alliance members.

The two Russians stood there in the entrance to the hidden cave, watching the chopper leave. Standing there beside them was one of their old arch-enemies, which had in recent years become their valued henchman. Osama spat in the dust, and then said, "Well, say what you like about Musharraf, but I still trust him only a little."

The more talkative of the Russians, the one which had conducted the conference, replied, "Do not forget that he is the grandfather of your own organization. Back when you were still a member of the Mudja Hadeen, fighting with every dirty trick you knew, against us Russians, he was starting his rise to power in Pakistan, and already had come to us with the first ideas about having his I.S.I. agents start up the thing later known as the Taliban. Without the Taliban, where would Al-Queda ever have found a sponsor, back in the early days?"

Bin Laden snorted disagreement, and answered, "He only did that because in those days Pakistan did not have nukes, or he would have just sent a couple of dedicated I.S.I. agents into a Western city with a suitcase nuke. After that, he could have led NATO around like an ox, with a ring in its' nose!"

The Russian snorted his disagreement, also, and said, "So, just who do you think gave the specs and blueprints for a nuke to the people of Pakistan, in the first place?"

Bin Laden turned and stared at him, speechless, and at last, whispered, "Why would you ever do that?"

The Russians both roared a huge laugh, and the other one said, "We knew there would come a day when we would want to control all of central Asia. What better way to do that, since we could not hold Afghanistan, than to make an alliance with Pakistan, and give them nukes, for a balance deterrent against India's nukes, and, then, later, those same nukes could be available to help us control all of central Asia, too!"

Bin Laden numbly shook his gray head, and looked blankly down at the floor of the cave, trying to fit all of the puzzle pieces together in his mind.

As he stood a couple of minutes, lost in thought, he did not hear the footsteps of the man approaching from behind. He suddenly heard a voice say, "You ought to know by now that you must deal carefully with these Russians!"

Bin Laden whirled quickly (for an old man) and saw Hamid Karzai standing there, grinning.

The Russians laughed again, and said, "Listen to him, Osama! We never forgot the lesson that Hitler taught us in World War II: always watch even your allies, until the war is over!"

The Russian continued, "Okay, the first chopper is out of sight, now, so go load up on the attack chopper, and it will race you back to Abbott Abad. We do not want the other delegates to know that you are actually staying in Pakistan, until the time is right."

Bin Laden nodded, and went to climb into the other chopper, which lifted off with him, and sped through the mountains on its' secret way back into Pakistan, to drop off Bin Laden quietly two blocks away from his secret compound, where a plain car met him, with tinted windows, and took him back inside the fortress.

As they had watched him fly away, the Russians also told Karzai to go get his little travel bag ready, since the choppers would come back soon to pick them all up.

When he was out of earshot, one Russian said to the other, "So, did you contact Al-Zawahiri, yet?"

The other smiled, and then answered, "Yes! He sees the advantage. Either he can take our offer, and take over Al-Queda after we have Bin Laden hit by the Americans, or we can come after him, and kill him, too!"

The other one answered, "Well, after all, he is the real master-mind of the group, anyway, and was always smart enough to stay out of the limelight, where he could work more effectively. He has actually been running things for over five years, now, and the old man has lost relevance, but his death at the hands of the American Seal Team will cause him to be of more use, as a martyr. It seems that our grandmaster in the Kremlin, Putin, has once again thought at least five years ahead, in this final endgame for world control!"

"What about Musharraf and Karzai?" the other asked.

The reply came, "All in good time. We can frame one of them for giving up Bin Laden, and the other one we can just kill, when the time is right. Each one has some present uses, but they always play both ends against the middle, and they cannot even trust themselves!"

Meanwhile, as the hours of Bin Laden's life counted down, the Earth, the moon, and six other planets wheeled majestically, and Divinely, into place, and formed a strange alignment. The heavy significance of this sign in Heaven would not be clear for a while, yet, but it was of much greater import than the death of one terrorist leader.

Adam and Eve, along with Wolf, and She-wolf, and several other graduated saints and famous warriors of the Kingdom of Heaven, all stood watching the spectacle unfold. They saw and heard everything that was happening, including all of the little secret whispers behind closed doors. Adam smiled, as he saw the final piece of the planetary puzzle slip quietly into perfect place, and he turned and looked over at King Jesus, Who was also watching it all with them. "Do any of them even notice the planets' alignment?"

King Jesus turned and smiled at Adam, and answered, "Yes, they have observed the event, but not a single one of them all, even among the Christians, can yet see the reason that I sent this sign at this time!"

EXECUTION

The intelligence arrived in early morning, as the men were just starting their day. Leaping up from their breakfasts, everyone scrambled purposefully about their last-second preparations, which were mostly things like jumping into body armor, grabbing the assault kits, checking ammo, and trotting to the mess hall again, for the final update and briefing, before launch.

The pilots and aircraft techs were going over the birds, tripe-checking everything that could be checked. If they had x-ray eyes, they would have been probing down into the polycarbonate material, instead of metal, of which the birds were built. These things were much stronger, and also much lighter, than any metal aircraft ever known.

The canine handlers were also checking over their mighty war dogs, since it would never do to send one into battle, if unfit. That might create a risk for the dog himself, and also for the humans depending upon his full strength.

As the commander briefed the men, he covered specific goals, extra instructions, and special cautions and priorities. The meeting continued until about 10:00 A.M., at which time the commander had the men to stand down, since the birds would not launch until almost sundown. Each man bowed his noble head, as they all shared a moment of sincere prayer, giving thanks, for being allowed to carry out justice, and that the time had come at last, after a decade of work and planning. They loved King Jesus, and would gladly risk their lives for a chance to serve Him, and to be His strong soldiers, and to fight for justice. They had all grown to know, and to love, each other as brothers, too, and each one would give his own life for his partners, but not if it meant failing the mission, which always came first with these men.

Each man returned to his own personal gear, checking and cleaning, oiling moving parts, checking sights, and doing whatever he knew he ought to do to prepare as completely as possible. Some of them spoke in small groups, some stayed alone with their thoughts. As the day waned, the men assembled again in the staging area, ready to board the choppers. This time, no one spoke, except the commander, and anyone he questioned. After a few confirmations of "ready", about the various aspects of the strike team, the commander led them all again in a final brief prayer, and then ordered them onto the choppers.

As the men boarded, the pilots fired up the ultra silent engines, and began checking all the green lights before takeoff. The men and dogs settled in for a long flight, knowing they had at least three hours to wait ahead of them. The younger ones, those in their mid twenties, had to work a bit to keep calm, and patiently wait out the time, but the older team members, in their early thirties, had enough experience that the wait did not bother them much. All of them were primarily glad to just finally be underway about this thing.

As the pilots brought their engines up to full power, the flight tech in front of them signaled all clear, and the lead chopper took off, followed in seconds by the second chopper. As they lifted off, the commander watched them go, and said another prayer for them, and a prayer of thanks for this wonderful day, which none of them had ever known for sure that they would see.

They already had been fairly certain about Bin Laden's location, but had only had it narrowed down to about a five mile radius. That was too large an area to infiltrate and control, if secrecy was required. Once the precise location was confirmed, the big boys at JSOC told the President, and, after a bit of "what if" type question and answer, the President approved the strike, and JSOC passed on the order, and the men loaded up and headed out.

The sunset lit up the tails of the disappearing choppers, as they scraped the Earth, flying "nap-of-the-Earth" style, using every hill and ravine as cover, to help avoid detection. This tactic was not actually essential, while still in Afghan airspace, but it would be a matter of survival, once entering Pakistan.

The two choppers hummed along low over the ground, cruising at over two hundred knots, which was still possible, until they entered the more mountainous border region. There they had to slow down, just to make all of the curves and maneuvers required to miss the mountainsides. On board each bird, the dogs had each fallen asleep, since they knew action was coming, but not here yet. Some of the men were lightly resting, also, but no one was speaking much. Some of the younger ones were still struggling to calmly wait it out.

A pilot, a co-pilot, sixteen SEALs, a dog handler, and a dog, plus a highly trained and experienced battlefield surgeon, were the full crews which were mirrored upon each bird. The pilots, the co-pilots, the dog handlers, and the surgeons, were all combat-ready SEALs themselves. Doctors could also shoot, as well as heal. One of the special instructions given had been to the doctors, to save not only the SEAL team members, but also Bin Laden, if he could be captured, but became wounded in the fight. If he could not be taken alive, then he would not need medical help.

Each of the soldiers knew what his specialty was, and just how likely that it was that he would be the individual one which actually killed Bin Laden. They had orders to take him alive, unless he offered any resistance, at all. If he pointed a gun at them, he was dead.

There were about a dozen of them total that would be the most likely. Among even these ultra-elite veterans, not all soldiers were created equal. Some were stronger, some were faster, and some thought more precisely, when immersed in a hot gunfight. Over time, the abilities of each of these men had been measured, assessed, and ranked accordingly. The very best able were the lead assaulters, and on each team, six men had the front door. Others handled explosives to breach walls and hardened doors, and still others handled over-watch, to keep any would-be rescuers from interfering during the operation.

One thing they all had in common was that they did not get all excited and nervous, just because they were going after the world's most wanted man. They were professionals, to the extreme, and they were able to compartmentalize their emotions, until this mission was complete. After that, they would have a beer together.

As the darkness suddenly deepened, when they entered the mountains, each soldier ran down his personal checklist once more. Many of them relaxed enough to do some deep prayer and meditation, although none of them fell asleep at all. Even war-hardened professional carnivores like these still felt, a tiny bit, like kids before Christmas, knowing the importance of this mission, and how good it would feel, just to finally finish a ten-year-long task! No matter that the final confirmation info came from a Russian double agent, as long as they could, and did confirm it, within hours, from a CIA operative on the ground, in Pakistan. Now, it was time to act!

They were still flying at high speed, but only at a little over a hundred knots. They were also still flying at very low altitude, just barely clearing telephone lines. They could see all the lights from the towns and cities below them, as they raced by in the night. A few people on the ground, still up and outside at midnight, heard the strange sound the ultra-choppers made, as they whistled through the night air. No one even thought that they were actually helicopters, with the weird noises they produced, something like a small propeller airplane, crossed with a very small Lear jet. The blades did not beat the air, as with conventional choppers, since they each had six blades, instead of two, three, or four, or even five, like the Russian super choppers. The Russian birds were very, very good, but the American choppers were vastly superior, in over a dozen different categories. They could eat the Russian birds for lunch.

In the deep darkness of the Pakistan night, the chances for clandestine arrival were very good, since these were stealth choppers, and they flew low, below radar.

In the deeper darkness, which hid the spirit realm from mortal eyes, opposing forces were also gathering very quickly.

The devil and many strong bad angels were trying to attack the choppers, and cause a mechanical failure, and they were also trying to assault the minds and hearts of the soldiers, to try to discourage them, and make them turn back. In addition to that, they were trying to break through the signal jamming being done by the good angels, which was keeping the Pakistan authorities completely oblivious to the whole unfolding operation.

As the two choppers full of men and dogs flew on through the night, the good angels started intercepting and destroying all of the missiles that the enemy angels were launching. The Holy Spirit Himself had entered the fight, and all of the soldiers flew on in confidence, becoming calmer, the closer they came to the moment of impact. They saw clearly that they were the guided missile which would lock target upon Bin Laden, and utterly destroy him, now!

Michael was already locked in a death-match with the devil, keeping it wrestled to the ground, and held tight, so it could not enter the fight directly. The evil angels were being beaten and hurt very effectively by all of the good angels, and none of the evil spirits was able to land any hits upon the choppers, or the men, since the Holy Spirit was guarding and protecting their minds and hearts.

As the choppers began to land, one of the pilots had a moment of doubt, which the devil and the bad angels saw, and immediately pounced upon. The devil could not wrestle free to do it itself, but one of the bad angels managed to cause a Bin Laden man upon the ground to launch a rocket-propelled grenade at the lead chopper, but one of the good angels slightly moved the chopper a little to the left, just in time, and the rocket hit a glancing blow against the rocket engine.

If it had been a direct hit, it might have destroyed the whole chopper. As it was, it just killed the engine, whereupon the pilot, returning to faith, immediately performed a quick autorotation landing, which saved everyone onboard from injury or death. As the chopper landed outside the compound, the second chopper set down instantly beside it, to recover all on board, and not leave them stranded.

The demons howled in rage and frustration, but the angels rejoiced, seeing the soldiers land safely. They had also seen that the great hand of Almighty God had actually settled the craft gently, since, at such low altitude, even the finest efforts by the pilot would not have had a chance to take effect. The chopper has to drop for a certain distance before the blades will rotate enough to enable a soft landing.

All of the men boiled out of the first chopper, carrying combat equipment with them. The strike team from the second chopper joined them, and the squad leaders decided quickly how to proceed. A third of the men were set to guard the choppers, and those others not needed for attack were loaded on board the remaining chopper, ready to go. The dogs were also kept on board, since they were best used for a true stealth attack, and, now, explosives would be required to gain entry. It would not work to have dogs running around while trying to detonate charges.

The explosives experts set the shaped charges against the fortified steel door of the compound, and then retreated around the corner with the rest of the team. Shouting a warning, the men set off the charges, which nearly deafened everyone within a hundred yards, and also shredded the steel door into about twenty pieces.

Within ten seconds, the dozen men that were the first chosen went into the still glowing door frame, and began to advance from place to place, staying behind cover, as they fired upon the few Bin Laden people there in the compound. There were fewer than a dozen people there, and only about seven of them were actually shooting back at the SEAL team. After about twenty five minutes, it was mostly over, with all of the defenders killed, at least, those at ground level. The SEAL team began to climb up the stairs, clearing the two remaining Al-Queda soldiers they found on the way up.

Within a half-hour of the landing, they entered the final top story of the compound, blasting through another hardened door. As they rushed in, they suddenly saw a woman with a knife rush toward them, and one of the SEALs shot her in the thigh. As she fell, screaming, Bin Laden's face suddenly showed around the edge of a door frame for a second, and then disappeared. The SEALs pushed forward into the room, where they saw him standing in a crouch by the bed, holding an AK-47, pointed right at them. Before Bin Laden could fire a shot, two of the SEALs opened fire on him, each with a single shot from their assault rifles, and he went down, dead before he hit the floor!

The men went over to him, nudged him with their boots, and then said over their helmet mikes that the target was dead. The squad captains then had their men gather everything they could carry, as far as anything electronic, such as computers, tapes, cd's, dvd's, flash drives, and printed material, as well. The amount of stuff they took was staggering, literally, as they raced to carry the many pounds of spoils down the stairs, and out to the remaining chopper. All of the team loaded everything they found of interest, leaving behind the wounded woman, although one of the doctors had taken the time to quickly treat her wound, and stop the bleeding. He also gave her a shot for the pain. There was no one else but her left alive there.

The men carried out the corpse of the accursed one, zipped into a biohazard type body bag. No one wanted the forensic examiners to have any trouble finding the cause of death to be an American bullet!

The explosives experts on the team had been busy with the fallen chopper. As soon as everyone, and everything, was safely on board the remaining bird, the pilot lifted off, and withdrew a short distance, about two hundred yards, from the compound. Then the order to scuttle was given, and the men pushed the detonator, and the fallen chopper erupted into a tower of flame that reached far up into the night sky. The blast made the earlier charges used for entry look tiny by comparison. If they had not attracted enough attention earlier, this ought to do it.

The squad captain said a swear word, as he looked though his binoculars, and saw that a chunk of the tail rotor assembly had survived the blast. They would not learn much, but their enemies would at least know something about the special material of which the bird was built, and the new and innovative tail rotor design would also be compromised. While they hovered, the captain had the pilot fire a missile at the thing, but it only scattered it farther away. He said another swear word, and then said, "Move it!" The chopper turned and raced away into the night. What they were carrying was more valuable than the loss of the tail rotor secrets. While the corpse of Bin Laden was indeed a treasure, the really valuable stuff was all of the material which they had recovered at the compound. Intelligence experts would be able to trace down and destroy most of the elements of Al-Queda, once the data had been analyzed.

The men rode in quietly satisfied professional restraint all the way back to Afghanistan. Even so, their rock hard muscles were very relaxed, and their rock hard faces actually showed the traces of little smiles. The smiles were very scary. Their faces resembled the noble warriors of Heaven's Army.

In the dim red light inside the chopper, the men looked like Wolf looked, right after he had hunted, and made his kill, just before he ate!

THE RIVER OF MERCY OVERFLOWS

As the people upon Earth began to find themselves in catastrophe after catastrophe, some of those, which had been granted wisdom from God, still continued to thank, and praise, and, yes, trust Him even more, despite all the disasters. Others developed hardened hearts, and began to blame God, and everyone who tried to worship Him, as the source and cause of all the problems. (These are the majority of Earth's people, which are too stiff-necked and proud to humble themselves before the Word of God, and instead, choose to have evil, unjust, selfish lusts to continue doing any perverted evil which they cherish. They delight in treating others cruelly, and in stealing things which they ought not to even desire.)

Some of them kept on calling the tornados "acts of God", which is a lie. (The worm was made to be the prince of the power of the air.) God sends good weather, sunlight, fresh breezes, rain, in proper amounts and seasons, and fruitful crops. (The devil sends destruction, disaster, and despair.)

After a while, it almost seemed like some sort of grim contest, as if the people might say unto one another, "My disaster is worse than yours!" (Human pride can even find a way to brag about tragedy.)

Adam and Noah stood beside King Jesus, watching with Him, as the mighty Mississippi River crawled through the valley, moving like a liquid glacier, scouring the ground under it, and drowning thousands of square miles of farms and homes, as it marched toward New Orleans. All of the frantic folks in the way of the torrent prayed and prayed that it might stop, or be averted, by some strange miracle.

Even though hand joined in hand, nothing that mankind could do was going to stop that flood. The people in Heaven could hear the groans and whines of the folks below, and did truly sympathize, but knew that the good Lord had a greater plan, to help the Earth, even at the cost of many farms and crops, as well as many folks' life-long homes. (The Earth-dwellers could not perceive the greater plan, since it is very hard to see beyond one's own emergency.)

Noah turned to King Jesus, and said, "Why do they not recall that in the days of the great flood, You were able, and willing, to save that part of the Earth which was acceptable for You?"

King Jesus smiled a little at the question, but before He answered, Adam said, "Yes, Lord, and why, also, do they fail to remember that You are the One Who delivers us from the power of the air, not destroys us with it? Why do they keep on blaming You, for all the evil done by the devil, and also done by themselves?"

King Jesus stopped smiling, when he heard the second question, and answered, "I know. It does grow tiresome. The enemy has blinded their eyes, their minds, and their souls, and turned their hearts to stone. Nonetheless, many of them actually delight in agreement with the devil, instead of releasing their precious pride, and learning the truth. They think, wrongly, that to agree with Me means they could never have any free will any longer. That's one of the worst problems with which we must deal during this Age of Faith."

"If they had read the account of our brother Job, they would realize that the enemy has some power over storms and weather conditions. They would also realize that I can, and do, still put limits upon the worm's activities, or else, the human race would all be dead already!"

Adam and Noah nodded silently, as they pondered the strange mindset of the Earth-dwellers. As they stood there, Job walked over to them, and greeted them, and stood watching with them, listening to all the folks complaining upon the ground. After a couple of minutes, he spoke, and said, "I guess they have forgotten last summer, when they all prayed that You would stop the oil spill, and restore the Gulf waters to clean health!"

King Jesus nodded, and said, "You are right. They did not understand that last winter's excess snowfalls were designed to help clean out the Gulf, once the snow thawed and made it downstream. By the time I have finished cleaning up their mess, most of the contaminants will be washed out into the Atlantic, where the Gulf Stream current will carry that poison all the way across the ocean to England, to bring the death chemicals home to those who released them into the water.

They also have failed to notice that only one person has died from this flood, even though it has been happening now for almost two months."

Adam nodded and said, "Yes, Lord, the original "accident" killed about a dozen, and your cure has only killed one!"

Noah joined in, "And even that one is a Christian, and was ready to graduate to Heaven, also!"

All of them fell silent a few moments, pondering the lack of wisdom in mankind, but quietly rejoicing in the mercy of our King.

After a few seconds, Job spoke again, "So, what are You going to do to New Orleans?"

King Jesus took a deep breath, and let it out with a sigh. He said, "It will depend a lot upon what they do in their hearts, while this is unfolding. Katrina got their attention, but they still returned to their strange ways, although much good came out of it, and many were saved, that otherwise would not have been, unless desperation had driven them down to their knees, where they at last turned to Me, for help."

"If they harden their hearts, I might not spare them, this time, but, if they humble themselves, and pray, and turn from their wicked ways, and seek My face, then will I hear from Heaven, and will heal their land!"

ATTACK OF THE KILLER TORNADOS

This year they seemed to be like waves of enemy bombers, striking without much warning, anywhere they chose. From Ft. Worth to Massachusetts, from Tuscaloosa to Joplin, no one was safe from devastation. These were big monsters, too, not just the run of the mill, ordinary tornado.

When the people saw them coming, they could not see the tops of the storms. The funnel clouds stretched from ground, to space, or at least the lower stratosphere, and blanketed the entire horizon in front of the terrified people, from all the way to the left, stretching all the way across the world to the extreme right, and they could see no edges to the storm, because it was that huge, and that close, just before many of them died.

Smaller storms produced the noise of a freight train, but these behemoths sounded like a full-roar jet engine, of a size like the moon rockets. The buildings were shaking just from the sound, many seconds before the 200-mile per hour winds slammed into everything, and began to rip it all apart.

As the tidal waves in Japan had carried along huge chunks of flotsam, including cars, buildings, ships, homes, railroad cars, animals, and people, even so the extraordinary winds threw anything and everything way up into the air, accelerating objects snatched from the Earth from zero to over 200 miles per hour, in split seconds.

Almost all of the animals and people which were so dramatically accelerated were also torn to pieces by the experience, as the strength of the demon wind tried to ignore the inertia of the mass of the living body. Few, if any, of them, survived the ride. Most of them were carried many miles away, or at least their fragments were, and they were never seen or heard again.

The trees fared no better, no matter if they had out fought the previous storms for a century or more. No matter how old, or how tough, a tree might be, these funnel-shaped annihilators were sent to finish a mission of total devastation, and that's what they did.

One of the biggest troubles the survivors had, at first, beside the numbness of shock, was finding which street was which. Street signs were gone, as were all landmarks, except for immovable terrain features, such as mountains and such. No houses were left, and no trees, and all that remained were hills of scrap, and broken trees, with bare slab foundations, and a few strong fireplaces, as far as the eye could see. Even once people identified the streets, they still could not drive upon them, until they moved all of the junk out of the way.

The enemy had been on a particular strategy to attack and weaken the U.S., by using a multi-pronged effort, including financial damage, emotional damage, spiritual confusion, stretching the U.S. military too far, and sowing dissention between the U.S. and many other nations, including, especially, Israel, and also, Pakistan, and Turkey.

The enemy knew that the U.S. stands with Israel, at least in military matters. The enemy wanted to weaken that alliance, to make Israel become more vulnerable to attack.

As with the storm in Tuscaloosa, the other storms were all sent also, by the enemy, and in the funnel of each one was a large demon, whirling around in a tight spin, spinning up the air into a deadly funnel cloud, and forcing the vortex down to the ground, to maim and kill. The mighty cherub, Michael, and the General of the angels, Tzedek-el, and many other strong, experienced angels met them on the front lines of the battle, every time. The demons were seriously wounded, some of them to the point of being made crippled, unable to escape. Michael fought directly, in the type of close order fight that men would call hand-to-hand, but, with a cherub, and a dragon (that used to be a cherub) hands were only a small part of the weapons which were available to such combatants.

When the devil sent a blast of hatred and depression and fear straight at the mind of Michael, Michael smiled widely, and did the mental equivalent of a casual wave of the hand to move a gnat out of one's face, and launched back a deafening blast of Psalms of praise and victory for the Lord God Almighty, God of Israel!

The devil visibly winced in sharp pain, and let out an involuntary little yelp, which made Michael laugh, as he said, "Fight fair, jerk, or I will hurt you very much!"

The devil, knowing that he was no match for any one of the three remaining good cherubs, struggled wildly to escape the unbreakable grip of Michael's right hand, while the good cherub was steadily punching him in the head, with his left hand. All the time, as the devil was screaming, and begging for mercy, Michael kept laughing, and saying, "King Jesus told you to knock this stuff off, and He told me, that if you did not, then from now on, I can take my sweet time removing you from the battlefield! I haven't even worked up a sweat, yet. Can you handle another six hours of this beating? Stop screaming for help, and answer me!"

Michael stopped hitting the worm, and, the devil weakly whispered, "Okay. I won't come back. No more tornados, this year. You have my word."

As soon as he said that, Michael stunned him with another mighty blow, this time to where the devil's heart used to be. As his hand latched into the devil's chest, deeper than any claw could rip, Michael said, "Your word is filth, worm. Instead, you will hear this Word from my Lord: 'Next time you cross a line which I have drawn, it will cost you more than you can bear. This is My final warning unto you!'"

When Michael had quoted King Jesus, the devil had heard the actual voice of King Jesus through the mouth of the cherub Michael. It had caused him to shiver violently, as though caught in a sudden freezing wind, which chilled him (to the marrow of his bones, if he had had bones).

Michael threw the devil away from the battlefield, with one smooth motion, a blur so fast the eye could not follow it, and the worm receded instantly, vanishing in the far distance, growling an angry snarl as it left.

The rest of the demons left also, following after the worm, in the direction

Michael had thrown it. There were some of them which were too wounded to escape, without help, so Michael and the good angels made some of the bad angels carry their wounded away with them. Even though the bad angels had turned evil, they still had the strength and recovery powers of an angel, and would heal in a few days.

The scars would remain upon them, as a reminder to stay away from the regions which the good Lord had reserved for Himself!

After they watched the last of them vanish, the good angels turned to the task of helping people and animals be rescued. Some of the folks scheduled to remain alive needed immediate angelic help, or they would die in seconds. Like streaks of laser beams, the good angels shot to where each of them was needed, in this case lifting a fallen brick wall of off a little girl, and her kitty, or catching a car still flying through the air, and setting it down gently upon the ground, or snuffing out a fire in a truck that the storm turned over, so the driver had time to climb out, and so forth.

Every one of them knew instantly where to go, and what to do, since they were in a direct "Mind-to-minds" link with King Jesus, and He opened His Vision unto them, so they all saw what He saw, and heard what He heard, and so knew immediately which were the most urgent missions of rescue, in perfect accord with His Own priorities!

Within an hour, most of the needed work was done, and the rest of the operation was turned over to mankind, as human helpers were beginning to arrive on scene. As the angels began to fly back toward Heaven, one of the younger angels asked the General, Tzedek-el, "Excuse me, sir, but why do we not simply bind the bad angels, and throw them into the outer darkness? There, they could no longer bother anyone, and they would remain there until the time of the Fire!"

As the angels flew still higher, mighty, beautiful wings moving in tireless rhythm, the General smiled, and answered, "Because King Jesus has ordered us not to do that, yet. We are to fight them, hurt them, and rout them from the battlefield, as our King orders it, and no more."

"Vengeance is His, and only His. If He sees fit to banish some of the worst ones, until the Fire, that is His call. There are many that are there already, waiting for the Fire, bound in darkness, in chains. We do that only when ordered."

"Beside that, no one can put someone in the outer darkness, except King Jesus, Himself. That is one of the abilities which He keeps reserved for no one else, but Him."

"However, our good King has revealed one interesting bit of knowledge unto me about this matter. There are already some

Christians upon the Earth, who have prayed many times, that our good Lord will begin to remove, and bind in outer darkness, as many of the evil angels as can be lawfully done, in each appropriate case. They want the good Lord to thin out the ranks of the enemy, so that we can have an easier battle ahead, at the final conflict. These strange little folks pray for great blessings, protection, and promotion, not only for humans, but also for us, the good angels!"

"The Lord has shown me that once two or more Christians agree, and pray for the same specific thing, then our King will begin to actually remove the bad angels, each one at a time, as He sees fit. The Lord will manifest this action, as soon as at least two united Christians, that understand, reach agreement, and both of them ask this of our good King Jesus!"

"There are also many millions of other believers which also pray similar prayers. The good Lord waits until at least two of them reach perfect agreement as touching any matter, and then He will act! This prevents a conflict of interest, say, if perhaps two Christians were for opposite teams in the Superbowl. Well, one of the two Christians has to accept a 'no' answer, or both teams would have to win."

After a few silent seconds of flying upward, while the younger angel thought about it, he quietly said, "It will not matter whether or not our good King removes any more of them, or not. We will still overwhelm them anyway, once He finally gives us permission to attack in full!"

Tzedek-el smiled at the young angel, and answered, "Of course, but it pleases our great King to allow His little brothers and sisters to help out in the war effort. They are not just pretending to help us win, using only little rubber toy knives, or little cap pistols. No, my friend, their weapons are very mighty, indeed, because He always hears them, and answers them 'YES!'"

Tzedek-el laughed a short, happy laugh, and went on, "Do not forget that the Children of Light wear weak, fragile bodies, and they do not heal quickly, like we do, so that makes them all instinctively fearful, if for no other reason, aversion to pain, and bodily harm! Nevertheless, among a very large percentage of them, in fact, almost all of them, the good Lord sparked a fierce courage, based on love and gratitude to Him. It burns hot in their hearts for Him, and even among us, the war-angels, you will seldom find a match for their bravery in battle!"

"We cannot die for Him. He has reserved that special honor for His brothers and sisters, since He once died for all of them!"

WATER MANAGEMENT

Noah, Job, and Daniel stood beside King Jesus, looking down from a balcony of the Royal Palace. As they watched events unfold, they saw, and heard, everything, including the invisible, internal thoughts and emotions of anyone down upon Earth. They were not overwhelmed with a deafening torrent of sound, but it was as if people watched a large crowd of folks down upon the ground, and could easily focus their tight attention upon any individual, or group of individuals, even mixed in with all the rest. Since mental and emotional links were also visible, the Heavenly observers could also see things like a dad and his son, far apart, geographically, but in close unity, as though standing right next to each other, in dimensions like heart and mind. Those, who were the re-born Sons and Daughters of Light, glowed brightly, shining their Heavenly Father's Light into the dark world around them.

After the Earthquakes, tornados, tidal waves, radiation leaks, droughts, and floods, and even some strange new disease outbreaks, even the almost-century-old H1N1 flu, it would seem that people would begin to try to understand the deeper motives in God's plan, instead of just looking up to the sky, and screaming, "Why, God, why?" Perhaps, if they took some time to read, and obey, His Word, they might find more answers, or maybe they might be granted the peace to keep on trying, even when there are no available "because" answers to "Why?"

Even though the natural man cannot understand the things of God, it is often difficult for even the re-born Sons and Daughters of Light to figure things out. Just because we all have the Lord Holy Spirit living within our re-born spirits, that does not guarantee that He will reveal every secret plan of Almighty God unto us, as if we have an automatic right to know.

As the observers upon the balcony listened, they heard many people giving thanks and praise, even through the devastation of the storms and floods, still blessing God for His goodness. They also heard many that spoke blasphemous things, and blamed God for their problems.

While they watched, the prophet Joseph, still looking as deeply tanned as he had during his days in Egypt, walked up beside them, nodded shalom, and joined quietly in listening with them. After one particularly insulting comment about God's weather patterns, voiced by people inconvenienced by the western floods (from abundant snowfall, producing once-in-a-century spring and summer floods), Joseph laughed a bit in amusement, and puzzlement, and said, "They still do not understand, even with all of their modern science and technology to help them measure, record, and learn wisdom?"

King Jesus released a deep sigh, and said, "Unfortunately, no, they still think that I am somehow neglecting their needs, failing yet to perceive the larger patterns. It is difficult to get them to think outside the box!"

Job said, "For us, Your long-time friends, it is easier to see that Your excess snowfall, all last winter, was meant to clean out the Gulf, from all the oil spill, to save marine life there, and likewise, this event happening in the western states appears bad, at a glance, but is instead a hope for the beginning to an end of the terrible drought all across the western U.S., and, if You had not done it, not only would the U.S. food supply from the Gulf have perished, but the main part of the breadbasket of the continent would have been lost to drought, as well. Only a few of them left alive remember the dust bowl of the 1930's."

Suddenly Noah laughed, a great roar of mirth, and shouted, "As if any of those folks knows what a REAL flood is like!" Everyone else echoed his laugh, except King Jesus, Who smiled a quiet smile, as He continued watching.

After a few seconds, Daniel said, "Yes, Lord, that was the best, and most accurate way possible, to clean out the Gulf, and replenish the parched U.S. with a single move, and even though people called it one of those strange seasonal things, we know it was a special mercy, sent by You! As melting mountain snow, it will flow down both sides of the Continental Divide, and into the Southwest, where wildfires have been raging in Texas and Arizona."

Joseph chuckled a small laugh, and said, "Even as they do not know what a real flood is, even so it just occurred to me, that as busy as I was trying to manage the resources of Egypt, to prepare for famine, how must more incredibly difficult must Your Own job be, to have to manage all of the world's water supply, and balance all the billions of tons of air masses, to produce just the correct weather result?"

King Jesus did not answer, but Job said, "Yes, and that is if the enemy does not sneak in and mess up something upon which You are working, as with the tornados in my own case, and also, recently, Alabama, Texas, Oklahoma, Missouri, and even Massachusetts."

King Jesus turned to look at them, and then replied to Job, "Yes, it was the enemy's tornados that attacked you, it never was an "act of God", as they lie, when they say that. Nonetheless, you know that the enemy never has been able to sneak anything past Me. Never. And, he never will!"

"No, instead, as with the excess snow and rain, I will bring good out of it all, and the worst thing that the devil could do will be made into the best things that I will do, instead!"

"Note the courage, faith, love, and strong hope, first in the Alabamans, then those in Missouri, and many other places. People grow, and stretch, when trouble demands it. Sometimes the growing pains are horrible, but the mature Christian soldier is what we're after, as Our finished product, and that is worth a lot of pain and cost."

King Jesus looked back down to the struggle upon the Earth, and He said, "For Me, it was even worth enduring the Cross!"

THE FIRST TIME I MET GWEN

Many long, long years ago, when I was
still young, and strong,

I met a girl, who changed my world, and
gave my heart a song.

I always heard people say the word
"dream-girl", and wondered what they
meant,

Until the day that she came my way, and
I knew she was Heaven-sent!

The very first moment that our eyes
locked, I felt a thrill of fear,

Then her voice spoke, time froze to a
stop, and I felt mysteries near!

Then her face (from my dreams) lit up
with a smile, and my heart returned to its'
beat:

I knew this girl was a treasure from God,
as she knocked me off of my feet!

WITH ALL DUE RESPECT

On Monday, July 11, 2011, the network broadcast of NBC evening news related a story about a funeral that had been held that day, in Brownwood, Texas. The funeral had been for a local firefighter that had tragically fallen to his death, while reaching a little too far to catch a baseball to give to his son, who was at the game with him.

The story received national coverage, and about 75 fire trucks, with their crews, came to pay their condolences, and to begin to take up donations for the fallen man's family.

Although they were completely unmentioned, in the national network news that evening, there were nonetheless three other funeral ceremonies also held, in the Dallas area, that very same day. These funerals were conducted at the DFW National

Veterans' Cemetery. The three men honored there were three homeless veterans, all of whom had served honorably, obediently, and unselfishly, in the strong defense and protection of their countrymen, even though no one cared anything about their lives, or their deaths.

Well, someone, maybe, did care, since the Dignity Memorial covered the costs for their funerals, including having "Taps" played, while other veterans stood by at attention, and saluted. These three men were buried with American flags.

Nationwide, it is estimated that there may be as many as 300,000 homeless veterans. These men and women are not crazy drug users, or psychotic street thugs. They are people who gave every ounce, of everything that they had, and could not even find enough mercy from the very folks which they had defended, that some bold employer just might have enough guts, to ignore the gloomy "economy" (which is just a cursed cop-out, when greedy cowards do not want to risk a penny of their own), to help a war hero, down on his, or her, luck. (Do you still wonder why some veterans are homeless? Then, man up, and stand up, and give them a job!)

The military Chaplain, who conducted the ceremony, was fighting back tears, as he told the story of one of the men, which, at the age of 50, had died alone in an alley, behind a liquor store. Poor health was the problem, not foul play. (Unless you also count it as foul play, that no one would hire a Marine veteran, with an Honorable Discharge.)

Now, obviously, we must honor our fallen firefighters, police, and other civilian first-responder type folks. But why does the nation continue to dishonor the military first-responders, which risked, or even gave, life, or limb, or eyes, or sanity? In case you did not experience this feeling yourself, we can personally inform you that it feels horrible to do your very best for your country, and return "home", to be disrespected, and treated like crap.

Wake up, America! Do you still wonder why your precious "economy" is still struggling, and keeping all of you awake, late every night? Maybe, try hiring people that helped keep you alive, and free enough to own a business, or else, continue to act like ingrates. Do you really think that Almighty God, in Heaven, does not see, and hear, and know, even your inmost "secret" thoughts? Do you not think that He will reward every man according to the deeds done in the body?

Make your own choice, and live your own life. What you sow, you shall surely reap! Show mercy. Receive mercy.

The great, mighty blessing of Almighty God was poured upon America, right after World War II, not just because they fought evil, and won, but because they rewarded their warriors, once they came home. Jobs were given to returning soldiers, new companies started and grew, and many millions of lives were built, and lived out, under that blessing.

Riches are not forever, and does the crown endure, unto all generations? If we want to have the kind of national blessings America saw, after WWII, the deplorable disrespect for our military veterans must cease!

Do not think that you will do any good, if you try to take a veteran to lunch. Instead, mentally put yourself in his place, and open a chance for him to work, so that he can buy his own lunches!

King Jesus ordered everyone to treat one another precisely the ways in which they wished to be treated. Disobey the King of Kings at your own peril!

THE LIAR-BREATHING DRAGON

The interview was not one that captured world-wide fascination. Although the subject matter was explosive to those in some regions of the world, the broadcast was aired in the U.S., so most of the bloody "jihad" maniacs around the world did not ever hear it.

On the news show 60 Minutes, Lara Logan was interviewing a man named Amrullah Saleh. Why? It was because that man had been the top spy in Afghanistan, and was in fact, the Chief of the Afghan Intelligence Agency, the I.S.I. Four years earlier, he had warned Hamid Karzai that Bin Laden was hiding somewhere in Pakistan. He had even told Musharraf that he could likely be found at a town named Mansehra. The Pakistani boss had actually lunged murderously at

Saleh, the moment he heard it, but was restrained from violence by Karzai. As it turned out, Bin Laden was indeed hiding only 12 miles away from Mansehra, in a town called Abbot Abad. If the hot tip had been pursued, four years sooner, it would have likely led to the location and earlier capture or execution of Bin Laden.

Amrullah Saleh had quit his position as head of Afghan Intelligence, since nobody would take his intel seriously, or act upon it. He came to the U.S., thinking that maybe the American public would listen more attentively, and act more wisely, than his own countrymen. For a year and a half, he had traveled around, meeting with government officials, sharing information, and urging the U.S. to take action, immediately.

Still, he was largely ignored, until Bin Laden was found and killed, by JSOC agents. Suddenly, everyone wanted to hear what he had to say, since no one else but Saleh had even been anywhere close to correct.

During the interview, Saleh clearly illustrated his belief that the nation of Pakistan, at every level of official authority, was about as two-faced and corrupt as it was possible for a nation to become. From the top, Musharraf, all the way down to the lower echelon bomb makers, which made all of the bombs used against the U.S. soldiers, the people of Pakistan actively hated the Western world, and in particular, the U.S., and Israel. The bomb making factories were hidden well, inside average little towns in Pakistan, not far from the border with Afghanistan. From there, the completed bombs were delivered to Taliban and Al-Queda terrorists, which set them off as roadside devices, or drove them into bases, if possible, or maybe destroyed a downtown hotel in Kabul, where Western journalists usually stayed.

When Bin Laden was killed, the U.S. had wisely kept quiet about the operation, until it was over. Pakistan had tried to hide its' complicity (in hiding Bin Laden for years), by crying out about the U.S. not sharing advance notice.

When the U.S., a few weeks later, had sent a small strike mission against the three "hidden" bomb making factories, the advance notice had been given to Pakistan, a day or so before the mission. When U.S. troops arrived, they found all three factories empty, with all the main equipment removed.

Saleh also reminded Lara Logan that Pakistan had been the one to sell nuclear technology to North Korea. Iran is working now to develop a nuke weapons capability, and a lot of their new motivation and know-how is being bought from Pakistan.

Pakistan did not long remember the kindness shown unto them by the other nations of the world, especially the U.S.

When the big earthquake hit Pakistan, the first nation in the world to send aid was the U.S. That is not all. Pakistan was regarded as an ally in the "War on Terror", but Musharraf had easily deceived Bush. He somehow said the right words, and smiled the right smile, and shook hands, just the right way, so that Bush believed Pakistan was on our side, instead of the truth, that Pakistan is one of our most deadly enemies. We have been paying them 2.5 BILLION U.S. tax dollars every year, since 9-11. This is to help them build up their military, so they can "help fight terrorism". Instead, they sponsor it!

It also puts a real strain upon the relationship between the U.S. and the entire nation of India, which is a major trade partner with the U.S. It does not calm your partner, when you give massive amounts of money to his mortal enemy, Pakistan. (Do not forget, India is also a nuclear power.)

Twenty or thirty years of change can make people forget things about one's past, sometimes. People forgot that Musharraf and his Pakistan intelligence agency started the Taliban. The intent had been to use the locals in Afghanistan against the Soviets. To this day, the Taliban can only act as much as the Pakistanis fund their operations, and equip them with weapons and bombs.

From the Taliban sprang Al-Queda, so, of course, Bin Laden and Musharraf were old buddies. Naturally, Musharraf was determined to provide more than just a desert cave for his old friend, when in need of a long-term hide-out. Therefore, Bin Laden was hidden in Abbot Abad.

(Instead of a dry, hot desert cave, Bin Laden had been living in invisible comfort, while being well protected, and well funded, by Musharraf.)

Abdullah, the king of Jordan, rolled over in his bed, a cold sweat dripping from his face, as he sat up in the darkness, and asked, "Who's there?" in a whisper. For a few seconds, there was nothing but silence, except for the sound of his own breath and thundering heartbeat, and the quiet, smooth breathing of his wife next to him, as she slept peacefully.

Then subtle things started to happen. A sharply colder breeze stirred in the room, moving the silk drapes a bit, and snuffing out the two large candles, so the room grew pitch black. Then slowly, a couple of feet in front of his face, another face began to form. It seemed to be composed of a sickly pale green vapor, and his nerves went tight, with goose bumps, and hackles rising on his neck, and chattering teeth, as he clinched his jaw and his fists, to try to overcome his terror, and at least, die like a king should die.

The face was human-like, but not at all human. There were things wrong, and things out of place. The face looked like it was made of carved granite that could move. The eyes were empty: dead, cold, black, empty, bottomless sockets, like a person without eyes. The thin lips were pulled back, in a "rictus-smile" of death, and the teeth revealed were those of a savage hyena, about to bite.

Abdullah wanted to scream, but could not move. He at least wished he could hit his panic button, hoping that his guards would arrive, and the thing might leave. Instead, as the face finished solidifying, and hung by itself in front of him (just a face, not even the whole skull, or any body below it), a voice like rough stones grinding harshly against each other came out of the mouth of the stone mask, and the thing said, "Oh, calm down, Abdullah. If I wanted to kill you, you would have already died. Now, hold still. I will show you some things happening around the world right now, of which you are not aware, and now you need to know. Watch!"

Suddenly, Abdullah saw Pakistan, and Musharraf, and all that he had said and done against the West. As the vision zoomed in to one particular meeting, where Musharraf and Bush were discussing just how much aid the U.S. was going to shovel into Musharraf's pockets, another layer was peeled back in the video stream, and Abdullah was able to clearly see the stone mask over the face of Musharraf, and the voice with which Musharraf was speaking to George Bush was the stone-grinding voice of the devil!

As Abdullah watched, fascinated, he heard the stone voice in his mind, saying, "Now, you know precisely who you yourself are: the direct, blood line descendant of my false prophet Mohammed, and the rightful, chosen inheritor of the throne of this world, and you will rule the world under me. As your ancestor Mohammed was my false prophet, so I now give one unto you.

Musharraf will be my mouthpiece of evil and lies, to deceive the West, and destroy them. I have been training him for this for over twenty years. Musharraf and Zawahiri will become your right and your left hand men. One will tell lies, and the other will engineer terror. Al-Queda will be world-wide, and will lead the charge against the West. Then, when the stage is set, and the moment right, you will lead all of the Islamists upon Earth in a world-wide war to end all of the West, and Israel!"

"Back in June, the leading council of Al-Queda, the Quetta Shura, "hidden" in Pakistan, in the town of Quetta, voted Zawahiri to become the new head of Al-Queda. I have already begun sending him new plans for terrorism, bigger, more deadly plans, and, so far, I am letting him think he is dreaming all of it up on his own. I want to build his confidence a bit more, before I show myself unto him."

"Now, look due north. See, past Syria, where Assad is about to be killed by his own oppressed people, there, hidden in Turkey, do you see them?"

Abdullah strained to focus his eyes upon small details in Turkey, but it was a lot of area to scan. Then, suddenly, he saw four huge shapes, as large as mountains, camouflaged in the terrain, looking like part of the landscape. As he watched, one of the mammoth things moved a little bit, lifting a head larger than a city, and locked eyes right with him, causing him to shudder, deep in his core of his frozen soul, but then, the thing suddenly smiled at him, and winked, then sort of rolled over, and went back to sleep. It resembled a huge orange dragon. The other three giant, hidden dragons had not stirred, but slept on. He could hear them all snoring, sounding like thunderstorms, a long way off.

The devil's stone voice spoke again in his mind, and said, "They are some of my biggest and strongest demons. They will sleep, until I wake them, and call them into battle to help you. They are on your side, but do not disrespect them, or they might grow angry!"

Then, the vision faded, and the stone face also began to fade, and the stone voice said, "I will make you my son, but you will do precisely what I order you. If you do not, I will kill the ones you love the most, and I will make you watch, while I torture them to death, right in front of you. Do you understand? Okay! Get some sleep, if you can. I will be in touch!"

At the last word, the face disappeared, and the retreating echo of the harsh laughter of the stone voice faded into the darkness.

FLINT

As they looked down from the observation deck of the Royal Palace, they each noticed a few bright, intense pinpoints of pure white light, scattered here and there, all over the entire planet. The whole Earth seemed cloaked in night, and there was no sign of approaching dawn to be found.

King Jesus was there with some of His friends, and they were all watching the scene below in a visual filter mode that showed the spiritual illumination of the Earth, instead of its' physical lighting. Once in a while, a new light would suddenly flare up in the darkness. As they watched, some of the lights blinked out, at times, individually, and upon occasion, several at once, usually when the group of lights was in close geographical proximity to each other. At rare moments, one or more of the little lights flared very brightly, flashing hope and inspiration all around, right as they winked out.

King Jesus said, "Now, see, there goes another of our men, flaring the bright light of a true witness, even under torture, in extreme agony, all the way unto his last breath! That gives hope unto others. See, a few dimly glowing little new lights are starting, right where they saw this mighty warrior die! Even two of his tormentors and murderers are being saved right now, because of his faithfulness!"

King Jesus suddenly turned and looked past all of them, over their shoulders, and, with a grand gesture of His hand, said, "Now, behold the man!"

As all of the folks turned in surprise, they saw a most unimpressive little boy, all of eight years old! He was a poor black lad, clothed only in a single cloth wrapped around him. The moment when he saw King Jesus, he dropped with his face to the floor, and began to tremble violently. King Jesus and all the other men there, about a dozen, ran immediately over to him, and lifted him up, calming and reassuring him, and giving him welcoming bear hugs, handshakes, and claps on the shoulders, with shouts of "Way to go, Mighty Warrior, champion of our Lord!"

As stunned as the young man had been a few seconds earlier, with terror, now, he was suddenly even more stunned, with wonder, and joy! He could not speak for a few moments, and then King Jesus shushed everyone else, so he could be heard, and he said, in a soft, sweet voice, "So this means that I did believe the right thing, then?"

King Jesus immediately grabbed him up in a fresh bear hug, and shouted, "Yes! Yes! A thousand times, Yes!"

After the fresh uproar had died down some, King Jesus went on, "I know that you were from Rwanda, of the Hutu tribe. I know that you believed in Me, and trusted Me, after one of My missionary couples came and spoke the Words of Life unto your village. I know that the world has forgotten the ongoing conflict there, since it has quieted a lot, but I also know that many of My people are there, on both sides, and they are being murdered for their faith in Me, even sometimes by their own tribesmen. In your case, I know that it was your own two older brothers that turned you over to the killers, and were therefore guilty of your torture and death. I said "were". The greatest witness about Me which you ever gave in your short, but beautiful, life, was that as you were dying, your brothers heard you pray unto Me, to forgive them! And, I did!"

The young man thought that his little heart would explode, from the overload of joy, when he heard that news! He suddenly looked eagerly right in the eyes of King Jesus, and said, "Lord, do you mean that they will be here with us, too?"

King Jesus smiled, as He set the young fellow down again, and placed a hand upon his little shoulder, and said, "Yes, they will. Not only that, they will help me to save your whole family! Not only that, they will help Me to start a tremendous revival, that will sweep across all of Africa, and into the Middle East! Millions of people will hear their testimony, and their story of your death, and faith, and they will turn many to the Lord!"

King Jesus then took the young warrior by both shoulders, and looked him right in the eyes, and then, placing His right hand upon the lad's head, He said, "Such mighty faith deserves a fine reward. From now on, you are a Knight of Heaven. I now rename you, and your new name is Flint, for when you were struck with deadly steel, you sent out a hot spark of Truth, and with it, I will kindle a raging wildfire of faith and revival, the like of which Africa has never seen!

Now, Sir Flint, please follow My friend Moses, and he will take you to the galley, where they will fix you anything that you want for lunch. Remember that I gave you the title of Knight, but you have proven to be, and will forever remain, My little Brother, too!"

THE GREEN HORSE GALLOPS IN SANDALS

Abdullah of Jordan slept less easily these nights. He knew that his neighbor to the immediate north, al-Assad of Syria, was just about finished. Even though a firm hand was sometimes required to govern properly, what Assad was doing was wholesale butchery, and it was clear evidence that change was coming, and Assad knew deep in his evil heart that there was no way to stop it. Instead, he tried to buy time, by means of mass murder.

Other revolutions had also happened, but with much less bloodshed, and much better results. The unique events of 2011 were changing the structure of the world according to the Mullahs. Before long, all of the Islamists in the world would think that they had a right to vote, and a say in how things were to be done. That development would never do, at all, for such men as Abdullah of Jordan. As kings, they needed to be in charge, even if dissenters had to be killed to retain their own personal power. (They know, deep in their wicked hearts, that in the future, they will burn for their evil.)

The outcome was not yet done, but it was almost certain to be over the day that enough of the military changed sides, and helped to overthrow the monster. When enough obedient soldiers of Assad had had to kill, or watch being killed, a sufficient number of women and children, and unarmed men, too, they would finally snap, especially if those they were ordered to kill were people they knew, such as family, or friends. Eventually, some of them would come to their senses, and turn their machine guns around, and destroy the tyrant and his remaining foolish supporters. It was only a matter of time. Critical mass would be reached, and chain reaction would follow, at light speed.

Abdullah tossed and turned in his restless sleep, and a dream began to form. It was a view of the world, and the nations, where Islam was gaining control and power, were glowing with a bright, but sickly, color of green. The precise hue of the green matched the green color seen in every flag of the world from an Islamic nation.

As he watched, fascinated, the patches of green began to spread, and merge, until almost the entire world was contaminated by it. All of the other parts of the world were mostly dark, except for where many intense, white hot little lights fought back against the darkness. When he looked toward the U.S., and Israel, the intensity of the millions of hot little white lights was overpoweringly dazzling, and his eyes slammed shut, to avoid blindness. He quit trying to look that direction, for now.

As he looked back at the green sickness, it began to writhe, and squirm, like an enormous, world-sized serpent's back. It heaved up in mounds, and then slammed back down, when encountering any of the little white lights, unless it caught a few of them, here and there, separated from the bigger groups. The lone individuals, and the small groups, it usually just captured, and then chewed them up, and then spit out the dead pieces. What the sick green monster could not control was that, as each little bright light snuffed out of this world, a flash of truth flared all around, momentarily stopping the sickness, and then a white-hot streak of light raced up to Heaven, from wherever the saint was killed.

The green sickness began to mount up even higher into the air, and began to form a giant green horse. The horse had a terrifying appearance, and looked impossibly wild and way too fierce to

ever be ridden. The moment the horse
had finished forming, it sent out a roar,
and the sound was that of a huge, world-
sized dragon, and a great torrent of flame
poured out of the maw of the beast, and
burned up a third of the world!

Abdullah was stunned by the vision,
and suddenly, he heard the stone voice
from his last nightmare, telling him that
this fierce creature was going to be his
personal mount into war. The stone voice
told him to look closely, at the hooves of
the horse. As he did so, the view seemed
to zoom in automatically, and very
rapidly, and he was able to make out that
the horseshoes were composed of
millions of little humans, all wearing
white turbans, white robes, and black
shawls across their shoulders. Every one
of them was marching along in
formation, but they were all running, full
speed, and they were all in perfect step.
They were all running in desert sandals.
As he watched, the soundtrack suddenly

cut in, and he heard them all, every one, chanting his own name, over and over, in unison!

While he was trying to grasp the full meaning of all of this, and reeling from the Technicolor, quad sound intensity of it, he "heard", or rather, thought, or rather, received a forcefully imprinted statement into his center of his mind, to the effect, that from now on, his secret new name was "Death"! He instantly blacked out, but the dream was still with him the next morning, the second he awoke, and he shivered in terror.

CHICKEN LITTLE WAS RIGHT

When he first woke up, his eyes would not focus, and he could not move around much. He found that he was encased in some sort of solid closet, or trunk, more likely, except that it was curved all around, with no corners anywhere. It was not absolutely dark, but was softly lit with a dim glow, brightest at the top half.

He tried to move his arms, to push against the wall, but he discovered that they were so tightly pinned behind him, by the snugness of the container, that all he could do was wiggle them a little. In desperation, he pushed his forehead against the wall, but it did not budge. In frustration, he slammed his face against the wall, and, much to his surprise, his astonishingly solid nose actually chipped a little piece of the wall away, and dazzling light flooded in!

He blinked his still unfocused eyes, at the bright light, but he wanted more of it. He kept slamming his tough nose against the wall, chipping away more and more pieces, until he could at last squeeze his head out. He saw blurs of white round things, lying all around him in the hay on the barn floor. As he looked down, he realized that the "closet" in which he had been sealed was also one of the white round things. Eggs!

Stunned, he frantically fought, as though mad, to finish his escape from the thing, and, a few minutes later, he broke out!

As he struggled to stand upon weak, brand-new legs, and to keep his balance, he looked down, and saw that his torso and legs and feet were those of a baby chick! That sight made him fall down in a shocked heap. After a little while, his numb mind began to try to reason through all of it. Soon, he gave up, and began to go "cheep, cheep, cheep", and to look around for food.

Over the days that followed, he noticed what he thought might be familiar faces hidden within the features of some of the other chicks. As all of them were inked upon the top of their heads, so that Tyson would be able to keep count of each and every chick, they were fed food with overdoses of growth hormones in it. They were kept in darkness, and never saw the light of day. This was done so that the chicken farmers could easily pick them up to slaughter, since the chickens would just sit down when it was dark.

Time did not seem to pass there, and eternity in hell seemed to be the destiny of these chickens. Because of the growth hormones, their internal organs could not develop correctly. Their muscles also could not keep up with their forcibly accelerated growth rates. In every chicken house, there were always more than 30,000 chickens, all crammed together in mass, all in total darkness, all the time. The entire floor of the chicken house was entirely covered in deep layers of chicken feces, all of the time. The temperature was usually around 95, in the summer. (Day and night.)

Sometimes, a chicken would become so weak, it would just fall over upon its' back, and lay there fighting only to breathe, and moaning cries unto God for help. For some reason, the good Lord, Almighty God, usually did not help, except to release the poor tortured creature into the peace of death. By that time, even such severe help was very welcome, from the chicken's point of view.

Upon some occasions, when the farm hands opened the door, to come in, and grab some full grown birds, and pick up the dead ones, a stream of bright white light flooded in from the outside, just for a few seconds.

As he was walking near one of the dying birds, he suddenly clearly understood what the bird was saying. It was praying for the good Lord to forgive it for all the evil things which it had done, when it was still a man, and not a chicken. The voice sounded very, very familiar, and then, suddenly, a flash of light from the door lit the face of the dying chicken, and he saw the face of his own beloved brother, who had also been his finest friend, and had also been his next door neighbor, and he had owned and operated the chicken farm just down the road!

He fell down beside his brother, as the full awareness of the whole situation came instantly into perfect focus. They had been chicken farmers, but now they were chickens!

Just before the door slammed shut, he called out, "Brother, Brother, it's me!"

The dying chicken turned his head, saw his brother there, and smiled, and with his dying breath, said, "I wish you had not come here, too. I pray our good Lord will also show mercy unto you, soon, and that you may be allowed to die, before they come to butcher you! I hope to see you in Heaven!" Then, he grew still, and did not move any more.

Suddenly, the farmer woke up, covered in sweat, having fallen asleep on his couch, after a long, hard day of killing chickens. He shivered, prayed, and then grabbed the phone, to tell his brother about the dream.

As soon as his brother answered, the farmer began to speak, rapid-fire, about the dream, and how much it had terrified him. His brother listened without a sound, all through the story. As the farmer waited for a reply, finally, he said, "Well?"

He heard his brother take a long, ragged breath, then clear his throat, and then say, quietly, "I know. I just had the same dream!"

FAITH-BASED CHOCOLATE CAKE

(Please have enough faith to try
this recipe!)

3 cups flour	2 cups coffee
2 cups sugar	2/3 cup olive oil
½ cup Hershey's Special Dark Cocoa	2 tbsp vinegar (distilled white)
2 tsp baking soda	2 tsp vanilla extract
1 teaspoon salt	

Sift, then mix dry parts, then add and stir liquids. Bake at 350F for 30 minutes. Use toothpick test, to tell when done.

THE SECOND SPACE RACE

The two Russian agents walked into the inner office of Putin, where he arose from behind his desk, and walked around to greet them, smiling about as genuinely as he ever did. He was actually pleased with them, and the way they had manipulated events in both Afghanistan and Pakistan. The desired result had been achieved, that Bin Laden was removed, and the Americans got the blame. After that, it had been easy to move Zawahiri into the leader position in Al-Queda. The Russians knew that he was far more deadly, intelligent, and dependably cooperative than Bin Laden had ever been.

Another of the hidden benefits included keeping the complicity of their agent, Musharraf, out of sight of the rest of the world. The world, in general, thought that Musharraf had been removed from power back in 2008. That was only the appearance. The Russians still called him either "general" or "president" when they referred to him, and they had a lot of respect for him. He had always been helping them spread their bargain-basement brand of nuke technology, to places like North Korea, and also Iran.

Musharraf had been the one sheltering Bin Laden, but gave him up, once the Russians had made it clear that it would happen, either way, and if he resisted, they would kill him, too.

No matter who was the official head of Pakistan, it was still a purely military country, and everything the government did was based upon the military's orders. Since long before the death of Benazir Bhutto, the military had only had one real commander: Musharraf. Officially, or not, he still ran Pakistan.

As the men sat down, and enjoyed a drink with Putin, he congratulated them upon their great success, and began to discuss certain things about the Space Station, and the dead Shuttle program.

"We know they already are designing, and have started building, not only the new VASIMR rockets, and are almost ready to test fire one, but they are already building the Ares rockets, for their new Constellation space program. They are racing us to the moon, again, even though we are not even in the race this time. Their stated purpose is for mining the moon, for helium-3, to return with it to Earth, and use it for cold fusion!"

"While that is plausible, and sounds good, I have become convinced that the actual mission is military, as a long-term base for huge gamma-lasers, which are the deadliest of all such things, and can send out a blast that will destroy entire cities or sections of territory, all in a single flash. The things require an atomic bomb to light up, and that destroys the laser, but not until it sends out something on the order of a solar flare. The moon is the ideal place to install, and use such weapons, since the foundation is stable, for ultra-precise targeting, and there is no atmosphere, so no spread of radiation beyond the blast radius."

"You understand what that means. Once they have even one of those monsters up and running, they will lock it on Moscow, and we will instantly become their property, forever. That huge a blast will make it all the way to Earth just fine, and burn right through clouds like they were not there. They will rule the whole Earth, for ever."

Putin fell silent, and looked out his upper floor window, wondering how long, before the first leaves changed color, and then looked back sharply, at the two super-agents. Then, he said, "That is why you must not fail. I will only have time to send one team, and we must gain complete control of the Space Station, before the Americans can launch reinforcements. You must overpower the Americans, as soon as the docking is complete, so they cannot send out any distress codes. Do not kill them. They will be good bargaining chips."

Putin silently looked out the window again, and a yellow leaf blew past. He smiled, and then looked back at his agents, and said, "It will not be too long, now. The X-ray lasers we are going to send with you are almost finished. They are plenty powerful enough to kill a city from orbit, and these things we can use over and over, after they cool down between shots. You will have four: three mains, and a backup. You will have to get one mounted, and wired, and operational, in less than six hours. We are designing them to enable you to do just that, along with their already calibrated targeting computers."

"Once the first one is online, you will be able to melt any missiles the U.S. tries to shoot up at you. The Space Station will let us rule the whole Earth, forever! But, we have to do it before the U.S. makes it back to the moon. We have less than three years."

Almighty God, the Father, sat upon His Holy Throne, and next to Him sat Jesus Christ. King Jesus asked, "Are You going to let them get away with that, Father?"

Father smiled, and answered, "Not entirely. That would mess up some of My final plans, and the specific things I will do before I send You back to Earth. Nonetheless, I will allow them to destroy the Space Station, since during the last few months, before Your return, I want them all to understand that anything which arrives upon Earth is from Heaven, not from men!"

HEADLESS CHICKENS

Abdullah of Jordan had a fairly wide range of ethnic groups living within his borders. Of course, the majority was comprised of his own folks, which used to be, up until the end of WWII, the people of Mecca and Medina, the guardians of the Black Rock. They were the only Arabians which could actually trace their blood lines back to the people of Mohammed, as in his own case, Mohammed was his blood line ancestor, and he was the rightful blood line heir to Arabia, and all of the territories of the entire Muslim world. All of the people of the Black Rock had been forcibly moved north, out of their ancient lands, and made to live in Jordan, and started being called "Jordanians".

The people which had lived in Jordan at the time had been there for thousands of years, and were the descendants of the

Edomites, and the Ammonites. Amman, the capital of Jordan, is still named for one of those two ancient peoples. All of that changed instantly, at the end of WWII, thanks to Winston Churchill. He was the one that decided to move ancient peoples around, out of their original lands, and the Edomites and the Ammonites were shoved over to the Gaza Strip, and started being called "Palestinians". There were still a lot of Edomites and Ammonites living among the Hashimites, or the people of the Black Rock. Abdullah was officially, and genetically, "The Hashimite", and was the only one in the world able to claim that title.

These days, there were also the Iraqis, which had fled from the south into Jordan, while the U.S. was bombing everything. There were a surprisingly large number of them. Add to them many Syrians, fleeing from the north, into Jordan, while Assad still cruelly repressed anyone unable to escape his paid murdering thugs, though the thugs wore official army uniforms.

There were some Iranians there, seeking shelter from certain madmen back home. There were many other types of Arabians living and working there, from various other tribes in Arabia. OPEC employees crossed borders with each other quite often. There were Egyptians there. There were people from Yemen there, too, most notably, the despised (by his own people) ruler of Yemen, which had been almost fatally wounded, and badly disfigured, by a rocket attack from Al-Queda, back in Yemen. There were some Libyans there, too, that had used to work for Gaddafi.

These folks all streamed through his mind's eye, as he lay sleeping, on a late August evening. As he began to wonder what the connection was, (except that they all came from other Muslim countries, and they all had some people

from there, here within his own borders)
he heard the growling stone voice speak,
or more like ram ideas and thoughts hard
into his mind, and he was helpless to stop
any of it, or even try to turn down the
volume of it. It was like being deafened
by the nearby roars of a jet engine and a
fire engine, while standing under a torrent
of icy water that was so heavy it almost
knocked him down.

Instantly awake, he rolled in his bed so
sharply that he launched himself out onto
the carpet, clutching his hands over his
ears, mouth open in a silent scream of
agony, and he began thrashing about like
a fish that was just landed. All the while
the flood of images and ideas still
overwhelmed his mind and heart,
drowning out any ability to protest, and
after a few minutes, he just lay still,
waiting for it to end. It was not the first
time it had happened.

The pictures, and the stone voice, told
him to note that all of the countries of

revolution, that had happened in the Muslim spring, starting in Tunisia, had been kept leaderless, without forming any solid new governments, in preparation for him, personally, to take over, and then, to lead them all into war. Even places like Somalia were being kept ungoverned, for now, until he was ready to assume total command and dominant leadership, of the whole Muslim world, including Malaysia.

Eventually, he would gather all of them against Israel, fielding a mobilized army of over 200 million. The Chinese would not have to send their entire military, which would leave them defenseless, back at home. No, he and all of his Muslim followers would be able to focus even more military power than China and Russia, by the time all of the plans were in place, or he would not be able to rule the whole world with an iron grip, unless that grip could produce a deadly stranglehold anywhere, any time, against anyone.

All the time his epileptic fit was happening, and the devil was invading his mind, his wife and the medical people were running in and tending unto him, placing a bit in his mouth, to keep him from biting and hurting himself, and injecting calming drugs, to slow the seizure.

The doctor told her that it would be okay, and that this trouble ran in his blood line, all the way back to Mohammed. It was considered a mark of greatness. None of them ever did grasp that when it happened to his blood line, it was being produced by demonic activity. Abdullah, like his ancestors before him, did not usually tell anyone what strange vision, or instruction, had been forced in, or what the experience had really been. Usually, they were too extreme, and terrifying, to want to recall.

The Heavenly Father, and King Jesus Christ, sat upon glorious Thrones of Power, and listened intently, to every word, and saw every image, as the thing happened. After it ended, King Jesus asked, "Is that why You caused them to remain ungoverned? I know that this was done by You, and not done by the lying worm!"

The Father smiled at Jesus, and answered, "You understand! Whatever the worm tries to do, from now on, until I send You back to the Earth, it will only work to accomplish My Holy Purpose. The worm will have no more victories upon the Earth, at least, not lasting ones!"

EARTHQUAKES IN VARIOUS PLACES

About the last week in August, 2011, an earthquake of moderate strength occurred in Trinidad, Colorado. About twelve hours later, another earthquake, of similar strength, occurred in Mineral, Virginia.

The rumble in the west only caused passing interest, since people in the west often felt minor earthquakes. The shock waves in the east were experienced with much greater fear and apprehension, since folks in the east do not usually have earthquakes as a routine thing. The buildings in the west were more properly designed for shaking ground, ever since San Francisco fell down. Most of the buildings in the west had been built after the 1904 disaster, and were able to handle more stress.

A few days after the two earthquakes, a massive hurricane named Irene began to head toward the east coast. It was interesting to note how the yankees responded so heartlessly to Katrina, but totally freaked out when faced with a little bitty category 1 storm, when it drifted into their own back yard. (They had responded the same way earlier in the year, when a rare tornado made it as far as New England.)

The same effect is usually felt, all over the world, whenever anyone watches a news film of disaster somewhere else. There is an expression that trouble never happens, until it happens to you.

It is easy to think in similar manner about people in our land who have lost jobs, homes, families, and futures. Those who still have such things often blame the unfortunate folks as causing their own troubles. The self-righteous implication is that they themselves are somehow superior people who claim to always work hard, and manage their money right, and deserve to rightfully have every possible material blessing. They never see the grace of God, or humble themselves enough to sincerely thank Him for the abundance of everything!

The first century Christians had a solution: everyone gave all they had, and there was enough to cover everyone's true needs, if not the latest cell phone, or fancy sports car, or big screen television.

So, just how sincere are any of us, in our attempt to honestly follow King Jesus? Do we really mean it, or do we just go through the motions, with shallow hearts?

I have a friend, and this friend of mine does a hard job, and does it well, but it is tiring, and does not pay much money. My friend budgets very carefully, and does without needed things, sometimes. My friend is a sincere Christian, and just sent a couple of hundred dollars to another friend, which is in the middle of an even greater struggle.

Remember that King Jesus told us that no one has greater love than to lay down one's own life for another person. Even if a couple of hundred dollars is not the difference between life and death, unto my friend, it means hope kept alive for the other friend, until times improve.

My heart swells with admiration, when I think of people like that. King Jesus also warned us that only the people that hear and obey His Words will be considered as His Own brothers and sisters. He will not tolerate hypocrites, or selfish people, not at His dinner table.

WOLVES SENT TO HUNT

King Adam and his finest friend, Wolf, sat upon the top of Mount Kailash, the Crystal Mountain. This was the unique pyramid-shaped mountain in the Himalayas, which wore a mantle of solid ice, which melted, and flowed down to form three of the greatest rivers upon earth. The water from those rivers sustained over 2 billion humans, and their animals, over most of Asia.

Adam and Wolf watched the people far below, as they practiced all manner of idolatry, and even worshipped the mountain upon which Adam and Wolf sat. The eyes of the people were held limited, so that Adam and Wolf remained unseen. (The locals counted the mountain to be sacred, forbidden turf, upon pain of death. Not that any, or all of them together, could actually injure Adam or Wolf, in any way.)

Suddenly, they both jumped up to attention, as they heard their names called, inside their minds, and the Voice was the One they loved most!

"Adam! Wolf!"

"Here we are, Lord!"

"I know. Get back here to the Palace, right now!"

Both Adam and Wolf instantly obeyed, leaping up into the air, stretching out their mighty wings, and grabbing huge chunks of air, as they accelerated upward. If anyone below had been able to see them, they would have looked like two streaks of hot blue fire racing up to Heaven.

A few moments later, they glided to a perfect landing upon the outer porch of the Palace, the observation deck, where King Jesus stood waiting for them. He smiled, nodded at them, and said, without preface, "Okay, so now I think it is time that we begin to thin out the enemy's troops a bit. Adam, I have special assignments for you and Eve, as well as for Wolf, and She-wolf. There will also be many angels sent along with each of you during your missions. These operations will be very important, and must not fail."

As He had been speaking, Queen Eve and She-wolf had trotted up beside them and each had nudged her own mate, just to say "shalom!" Also, Prince Abel had joined them, quietly.

"First, Wolf, call all of your kin, which lived once upon Earth, but now live here with us!"

Nodding his great head once, Wolf threw his majestic howl out to the farthest reaches of Heaven, shaking even the walls of the physical universe a little. A few seconds later, echoing howls came in from all over the sky, in every direction! As they watched, millions of Heaven's Wolves appeared, flying toward the palace from all quarters. Like Wolf, and She-wolf, these fellows were huge, towering at about 12 feet high, while sitting down! Even polar bears and grizzlies would run in terror from them, and most dinosaurs would, too. Only the T-Rex was vicious enough, and stupid enough, to try to fight something like the wolves of Heaven. (T-Rex would lose the fight, anyway.)

While the wolves were gathering quietly, waiting for orders, millions of war-angels, fully equipped for battle, also flew in, and settled behind the mass of wolves, and they all waited respectfully, to hear whatever King Jesus wanted to tell them. The war-angels stood about fourteen feet tall, about the same as King Adam, and Prince Abel. (Queen Eve was a little bit shorter, but she wore it very well.)

As the entire assembly finished forming, King Jesus raised His Voice, and said, "Now, these are your orders: Adam, you and Wolf will seek out and harass the worst rulers upon Earth, continually disrupting the plans, and the power structure, and the chain of command of the enemy. Give the worm no peace, and meddle with its' evil designs constantly. You will have with you all of the angels you need!"

Next, King Jesus turned to Queen Eve, and said, "Eve, I want you and She-wolf to hunt out the worst females in the Earth, and do likewise unto them, and all of their evil schemes, as I instructed Adam. Fight the humans, and the worst of the female animals, too, but leave the battles against the demons for the good angels, which will escort you wherever you travel."

Then King Jesus turned to Prince Abel, and said, "Abel, since you were the first-born child of faith upon Earth, because your dead brother was disqualified, your assignment will be to seek out and stop the most dangerous and destructive children upon Earth. 'Even a child is known by his doings, whether they be pure, and whether they be right.' So, seek out and stop those that pose the greatest danger, and, if their hearts can still be turned, I will spare them. Nonetheless, stop them before they commit a deadly sin, which I might not forgive!"

Then, King Jesus swept His fiery Eyes across all of the wolves and angels there, and He commanded them all, in a very strong Voice, "Now, you have heard My orders to Adam, Eve, Abel, Wolf, and She-wolf. All of you will escort them, defend them, perfectly, and press whatever attack they deem necessary. Let none of the enemy escape from a battle. Kill the evil humans, and I will judge them later. Kill the evil animals, and I will judge them later. Good angels, arrest and bind the ring-leaders among the evil demons, and, upon My authority, cast them into the outer darkness, in chains, to await the time of the Fire!"

"As you complete your missions, keep the eyes of Earth from seeing you. I do want the demons to see you, just at the moment that you hit them like a ton of bricks!"

"Since they like to frighten My little brothers and sisters so brutally, let's see how the twisted demons like it when they cannot see the punch coming!"

THE HOMETOWN OF EVIL

Most people in the western world had never even heard of the place. It was a strange little town, in a strange little country, and that made it easy to hide in a huge flashy world, full of big countries, and big cities, and big, noisy things happening, all the time, everywhere.

That was one of its' primary advantages, and why the al-Queda had set it up to become their secret headquarters. It was also conveniently close to the Afghan border, which made it easy to smuggle people and bombs into Afghanistan. Since it was located in the south west region of Pakistan, and remote from the large cities, and crowds, only rugged roads connected it to the outside world. Unknown, well-camouflaged, and disregarded as unimportant by most of the world, the town of Quetta had lived an invisible double life, concealing the monsters lurking within it.

As of lately, however, JSOC and the ISI had concentrated their surveillance and infiltration efforts there, having discovered that Zawahiri had been elected to replace Bin Laden, one month after Osama's death. The people (which had done the electing) were the "Quetta Shura" (the ruling council of al-Queda, worldwide).

In the first dew days of September, 2011, the U.S. told Pakistan where they could find, and arrest, a very key member of al-Queda, and two of his top operatives. The man they were after was Yousin al-Mauritani. They got him, on September 6th. The next day, on September 7th, a bomb set off by al-Queda killed almost thirty people, in an attempt to kill the local high ranking military officer that had conducted the previous day's arrests. Many innocents died in that revenge-bombing, but the terrorist mastermind, and his two best agents, remained in secure custody, unable to plan any further destruction against the U.S.

From this point on, it would not be possible for Quetta to be a secure base of operations for the monsters. The hornet's nest had been knocked down. The problem now was just a deadly bunch of angry hornets, swarming desperately around, trying to sting everything in sight.

The Lord Jesus looked down upon the world, scowling in disgust, at Quetta. Joshua, Caleb, Gideon, Samson, David, and the Macabbees were standing beside King Jesus, watching Him think. After a few minutes, Joshua, the great conquering general of Israel, as they captured the Promised Land, mustered up enough boldness to ask, softly, "Lord, do You want us to go destroy them for You?"

King Jesus answered Joshua, after a few more seconds of thought. He said, "Not just yet. I am planning to take the evil those twisted monsters are trying to do, and change it into something wonderful, and good, instead! Right now, I will let them regroup, somewhere else, and think themselves strong once again, so they can help the deceiver confuse the nations. This is all precisely what is woven into the unbreakable prophecies of Scripture. As I live, My Word shall not return to Me void!"

OUT THROUGH THE IN DOOR

All right then, just where does it go? When a soul leaves a body, what happens? From the Scriptures, we know that the soul of a beast returns to the Earth, from whence it came. From the same Scripture, we know that the soul of a man returns to God, from whence it came. We also know that man only has a "borrowed" soul. Only those born again of the Holy Spirit are given ownership of their own souls, after that.

Einstein was indeed brilliant, but he missed a couple of points. His mathematics broke down, when he tried to express a mathematical model of what happens inside the center of a black hole. Since that is a region of reality where all of the rules of physical space and time are radically modified, normal mathematics, however advanced, cannot precisely describe what is actually in progress there. Einstein did not accept the existence of black holes, even though his own math indicated that they must exist. He rejected the whole concept as "too weird".

A century after Einstein, we now know that there are truly black holes, and that the giant ones are all located at the very center of every galaxy, and that it is the extreme gravitational field of these monsters that forms the galaxies into the spiral and elliptical shapes, depending upon the mass and speed of revolution of the central black hole.

We also know about quasars, mysterious ultra-monster sized things at the outmost reaches of reality. Although impossible to accurately measure much about them, we know that they are extremely massive, but still manage to output billions of times more gamma and radio emissions than it should be possible for a single point source to emit. No matter how refined the optics have become, we still only dimly perceive those strange things, that are as bright as a very large galaxy, but generate more juice than billions of galaxies, with each quasar spewing out way too much radiation, and they must not be considered within the normal context of the usual, run-of-the mill galaxies or super-clusters.

Without all of the modern clues we have, to help solve these mysteries, Einstein really could not see the connections. He never knew that quasars existed, and he never realized that the black holes and the quasars are directly related, even closer than next door neighbors. They are more like roommates, or maybe even a type of galactic Siamese-twin set. The stuff being forced, by unbelievable gravity concentration, into the black hole, has to go somewhere. Matter cannot be destroyed, only converted into energy.

The quasars have to be generated somehow. A huge burning ball of fire and radiation does not just magically appear, here and there, always at the outmost extremes of the universe. No, something is making them form out there.

Now, here's the connection: all of the energy cramming down into the black hole rips open the structure of space and time, and the force of the shockwave drives the explosion of energy as far out from the center of the universe as it can bounce. It is likely a type of safety valve built into the structure by our good Lord, so that the concentrations of mass and energy will not produce havoc with the stability of the dimensions and the timeline of reality.

Now, if you are still in step with my thoughts, I will relate a strange event, which happened back in September, 1993, and is the perspective which began to open this connection to be understood.

A similar thing may happen, as a soul leaves the body.

We know that a human body loses approximately six pounds, at the precise moment of death. What is it that weighs six pounds? Where does it go?

It was a wonderful Saturday afternoon, and football season was well underway. As usual, I had a game playing in the den on the television. (It may have been Alabama playing someone else.)

As I watched the game, I took out a frozen pie from the fridge, and took a steak knife, to cut open the plastic wrapper around the pie. It was thicker plastic than I thought, and the knife slipped a little, and sliced deep into the side of my thumb, near the tip. (The thumb nail stopped the blade from going all the way through.)

I washed it with water, and then poured on peroxide, then more water, then, more peroxide, until it was bleeding slow enough to press it closed, and hold it for a few minutes, while I used the remaining fingers to open some gauss and a band-aid. After some patchwork, the thing settled down, and I put the pie back in the fridge, and went to sit down, to slow down my heart rate. As I walked down the hall, to my room, I was suddenly aware of a massive tiredness, reaching all through my whole being, including my body, mind, heart, and spirit. I was just so very tired, that all I wanted was to rest.

I missed my Dad. He had passed about a year and a half before that, and my Mom had already been gone for about six years before that. I had my career, but all my relatives lived hundreds of miles away, and I had learned how to live very much alone, and was plain tired of it all, and lonely for my folks. Instead of sitting in my big chair, I stretched out crosswise, across my bed, with my head toward the east, in the direction of Jerusalem.

Then, for the first time in my life, I prayed for the good Lord to just let me come on home to Him. I told Him that I missed my family, and was tired, and did not see any need to stay on the Earth. I had already done more things by the age of forty two than most folks get to do in a whole life. It was about two in the afternoon.

I remember relaxing, and withdrawing, inward, NOT downward, but into the very center of my awareness. My perception of things outside myself began to fade. In a few seconds, I could only hear my own heartbeat, and the sound of my breath going in and out, calmly. I recall how peaceful everything was, and how calm, and quiet, and dark, but not scary dark, just warm, comfortable, peaceful, restful darkness and silence. I withdrew further into the quiet, dark center, and released everything in this world, along with a long, slow breath.

The next thing I recall, I was sort of being fit back down into my body, sliding down into it like a hand into a glove, right through the center of the top of my head! Somehow, I knew I was coming back down, not back up from below. As awareness of my body, and the outside world, returned, I took a deep breath, and realized with a shock that my body had not moved even a fraction of an inch, for the entire hour or so that I had been gone! The precise position upon the bed was identical to the position I remembered when I had let go the last, long breath, down to the smallest detail. It was like my flesh had been held in frozen time, for about an hour. I cannot explain this, but somehow I am quite certain that I had not breathed a single breath during that whole hour.

No, I do not have any memory at all, of anything that may have transpired during that hour. I have given up trying to remember, since I suppose that I am not allowed to do so. Maybe one day the good Lord will open my memory of it.

At times, I wonder if I really did die, or if something else happened. I know the good Lord did not let me stay gone. I do not know if He sent me back, because He wanted me to do something more, like maybe write these books, or maybe He just thought that I was too immature and unpleasant to be admitted into His company for a permanent stay. I am quite sure that He had His Own valid, just reasons, whatever may prove to be the case.

It does puzzle me, however. I wonder why He would not just kill me, and keep me dead, if He felt anger toward me. I also cannot fathom why He sent me back, unless He felt anger toward me. (Who would rather be here, instead of there?)

Therefore, for the last eighteen years, I have tried to focus upon that memory, of the sensation of coming back DOWN, into my body, instead of back up. I have some hope that maybe He will finally let me come back up, if I ever finish whatever He made me to do. (Also, yes, if I was not scared of God before that, you can bet that I am now!)

ADAM'S FIREPLACE

The man had come a long way to search and study these mountains and rocks. He was a Christian Hebrew, born in the U.S., but now living here in Israel. The less well known and explored remote regions of the countryside were those which drew his interest. Also, the more rugged the terrain, the better he liked it. The things which might still be hidden, awaiting discovery, would not usually be found in the more well known and frequented areas.

He had grown up as a Christian, by faith, and re-birth, since the age of eight, and also, he had grown up as a Hebrew, by genetics, even more than by strict Hebrew upbringing. His folks had been very intelligent, well-educated, strong, gentle people. They had never denied their Hebrew heritage, but they were also born-again, and understood that the

Hebrew part was extremely important, but that the parts about King Jesus Christ were the most important subjects that existed, anywhere, or any time.

Intense study of Scripture, and intense interest in archaeology, had led him to follow the tug in his core of his heart. Israel was where the ancient past had actually meant something that mattered, as far as God's interaction with mankind. There were other places that mattered as well, but usually for one time events, like the tower of Babel, in Iraq, and the Red Sea, and Mount Horeb, in Midian, where God gave Moses the Two Tablets of Stone. By far, the greatest concentration of significant historic events (major things), which affected the entire human race, and the future destiny of mankind, always had happened in Israel, and they always would. He had to search the rocks of Israel.

He had been in the mountains, not too far from Jerusalem, but in some of the most rugged terrain there. He was exploring, and camping, alone, armed with his rifle, and machine gun, and pistol, and knife, and cameras. He also had a satellite phone, and cell phones, and a radio. This was so much to carry, that he had been forced to buy a little gray donkey, and persuade him to help with the equipment. In addition to the donkey, a huge wolf-shepherd hybrid bounded along, ahead and beside him. He had government permission, and permits, since he was known as a professional archaeologist and researcher, and also had become a contract consultant and professor at the University of Tel Aviv.

This particular morning, he and the wolf and the donkey worked their way along a steep ridge, climbing higher up, as they watched their footing carefully. Up ahead, he thought he saw a little wider spot, but could not tell from the lower angle, if there would be more room for them to stop and rest for a few minutes. This area was mostly deserted, since the rocks grew no crops, and did not seem to contain anything like gold or silver. The elevation was not high enough for snow.

They arrived, huffing and puffing, at the wide spot, and found, as they came up over the edge, that it was indeed a level place, almost twenty feet wide, and about sixty feet long, and they slumped down, all of them, and panted for air in the cool morning sun. The view was grand, and offered a nearly 360 degree view of the local countryside, for as far as maybe thirty or forty miles in some directions. The breeze was fresh, but not freezing. A golden eagle flew high overhead, and his cry echoed around the hills. They all looked up at the eagle, as they stretched out and rested.

A few minutes later, the man stretched his back muscles, and rolled in a twisting motion to his side, to fully stretch all of the muscles and spine. As he did, his eye saw something strange. He instantly sat up, his fatigue gone in a flash, as his heart raced. He moved over to the thing, and began to take several quick photos, and then he began to carefully brush away the dust, and the encrusted rock and dirt around the artifact.

The donkey and the wolf watched, content to rest and wait. The wolf thought that the man had found a buried bone that he fancied. He was not too far off.

After more than an hour of careful, painstaking work, and a ton of digital photos, the man had cleared away the concealing crud, and sat looking at two small chips of flint, no longer than four or five inches. They were too large for arrow heads. No bow except an English longbow, or a crossbow, could ever have hurled a giant arrow head like that. Since those had not been present in ancient Israel, they could not be arrow heads.

They were likewise too small to be effective spear heads. Perhaps, on a small spear, they might work, but on a serious war spear, or even a serious hunting spear, the stones would be too light.

He stopped, took a long, slow drink of water, and ate a quick energy bar, while his mind raced, and he gave thanks in prayer, for the miracle this day had revealed. (Later tests would prove that his find had the time accurately gauged at 780,000 years B.C., making it the most ancient human artifact ever found upon the Earth!)

After another two hours of work, during which he had to feed, water, and tend to the animals, he managed to record every possible aspect of the find, including all G.P.S. data, the weather, the precise time and manner of the discovery, and so on. Then, he unpacked his laptop, typed up a detailed, but brief report, and sent it to his colleagues at the university. The reply came back in about fifteen minutes. They wanted him to proceed, and retrieve the items, for laboratory study.

He acknowledged, and then breathed a deep sigh, and said a serious prayer, to calm his nerves, and his hands. Then, he slowly reached out his fingers, to gently, lightly, like a whisper, brush the nearest of the two stones. The moment his skin touched the stone, things changed!

Suddenly, he was immersed in night, with a bright, full moon shedding enough light to dimly make out the ledge, with only deep black void beyond the rim of the little plateau. The stars were extremely intense, and the air smelled cleaner and denser, and seemed to energize him more each time he took a breath. As his eyes began to grow used to the dark, he gasped a quiet, muffled breath, and dropped like a rock to the ground, in a flat, prone position. He dared to look at the things that had shocked him. Down near the other end of the little ledge, he could make out figures in the dark. At first, he thought that they might be the wolf, and the donkey, but they were nowhere to be seen.

What he saw there were two humans: a large, strong looking man, and a smaller person beside him. There were wolves also there, all right, but there were two of them, and they were enormous! They seemed to be a part of the human's family, or something.

The man held his breath, afraid to move, or make a sound. The strangers might kill him, if they saw or heard him there. And how had things gotten dark so fast? Had he hit his head, and been lying there unconscious, for hours, until night fell? And why had the strangers not already seen him, unless they had arrived after dark, which made little sense, considering how crazy a person, or animal, would have to be, to walk along this dangerous ridge, without light to see. Even with a full moon, that would almost certainly be fatal.

Suddenly, the larger wolf, the one next to the man, snapped his head around, ears up, and focused, nose quivering, and lip curled back, as a low, deep growl came rumbling out of the chest of the wolf. He sprang lightly to his paws, and trotted, alert, toward the hiding man. The wolf stopped a few feet away, and picked up a couple of big sticks, and trotted back to give them to the man at the far end. The man laughed, and said, "Okay, Wolf, so you proved me wrong again! Maybe we can find enough small brush up here, from old dead trees and such, and maybe we can cook and stay warm tonight, too. Good boy!"

With that comment, the man also got up, and followed Wolf back toward the archaeologist, who rolled to find a better hiding place behind some small boulders off to the side. There was just enough room for him to hide there, but only a foot or two to spare, before he would fall over the edge. He had better not roll the wrong way, if he fell asleep!

After a few more minutes, Adam and Wolf had been joined by Eve, and She-wolf, and all of them had gathered whatever small sticks and bushes they could locate. Adam stacked them carefully into a little log-cabin-style fire, and then he gently pulled out some of the lose under-fur from the thick coats of Wolf and She-wolf, and made a little spark catcher pocket, right in the center of the sticks. Then, he began to strike the two little flints together, sending sparks down into the nest of wolf fur, until a little glow started. It was just a tiny little orange smolder, at first, but Adam leaned down, and softly breathed a steady stream of air into the growing glow. A little later, a bright yellow flame leaped up as the fur nest ignited, and then grew quickly brighter, as the smaller twigs caught quickly, and began to also light the larger sticks. Adam stood back, and watched the fire grow on its' own momentum.

Meanwhile, the hiding archaeologist stared at the faces of the two magnificent humans, and the stunningly beautiful faces and forms of the wolves. He had never seen any creatures more beautiful, in his whole life. Each one of them seemed to be the flawless, perfect prototype of man, woman, wolf, and girl wolf. The people and wolves cooked and enjoyed their meal, and then, they all snuggled up together, close to the fire, with the rocks, where the man was hiding, to their backs. The archaeologist felt like he was intruding, although, short of jumping to his death, he could think of no way to exit the plateau. He curled up against the rock at his back, and fell asleep, staring out into the night, beyond the edge of the ledge, counting stars, while he gave thanks, for the strange and wonderful things which he had seen this day. He still was not sure how he got here, or what year it might be, or how he might ever return back. He had no doubt, somehow, that the people sharing the ledge with him that night were the actual, original Adam and Eve, parents of all of mankind. They were not dressed like cavemen. Adam and Eve wore the finest hand crafted buckskins, with similar boots and fur great coats, with hoods. They carried with them buckskin gloves, snowshoes, a type of rough ski pole for each hand, water skins, and some dried food provisions. Apparently, they were planning to head even further up into high country, maybe to winter in a cave they had found previously. Adam wore a dagger that could only have been carved from a tooth of a T-rex. Eve wore one, also, just a smaller version to fit her hand well.

When he woke up, it was not yet light at all. It must have been about 4:30. He looked over the rock, and saw that all of them had gone. The fire still smoldered, but was only hot coals and ash, now. Still, he thought, since no one else is using it, and it is chilly this morning, so, why not?

He climbed over the rocks, and sat down close to the fire. As he thought about all of it, he noticed something in the dirt, near to the fire. He brushed the dirt away, and fell back a couple of feet in shock.

There, right in front of him, in precisely the same position, spot, and arrangement, were the two flints. Adam had left them there, and no human hand had ever touched them again, for almost 800,000 years! Trembling, he reached out his fingers, just to lightly brush the flint nearest to him, not even sure if he was hallucinating, or not.

Instantly, he found himself back in modern times, looking down at the flints, with his fingers just an inch away from them. He yanked back his hand, afraid to touch the stones again, without a glove.

He carefully retrieved them, and loaded them into his backpack. These he would not trust to be carried by the donkey. If the two flints were lost, he could not endure the loss, anyway, knowing what they were, and to whom they had belonged, before the world began.

CON-MEN IN THREE-PIECE SUITS

It sort of reminds one of the old saying, about how no one wants to mention the elephant standing in the middle of the room. (The elephant in this example is not intended to represent any political parties of any kind.) Of course, the motivation for maintaining an unrealistic silence about a difficult or even crisis situation is usually embarrassment, for those responsible for the presence of the elephant, but it can also be that keeping the elephant there in the middle of the room is making someone a lot of money!

I remember growing up in an America where people could find work, and plenty of it. The U.S. still has enough population, infrastructure, activity (of all sorts), and financial wherewithal, to be able to make jobs for people, as jobs once were made plentiful.

There are still plenty of big companies, and big investors, that could power a new wave of homegrown jobs and products, if they only would. Big business blames the "economy", but keeps on sending thousands of jobs overseas: to China, and India, and South America, and many others. Investors taught them this trick, many decades ago, when stashing large sums of money off-shore, and far abroad, to avoid taxation.

To folks like that, the bottom line is vastly more important than behaving like a true citizen of the U.S., and keeping the jobs at home, where they could be of great help, to our fellow countrymen! One possible description of this shameful behavior might be "international selfishness". Or, we could call it by its' common name: "greed".

Big business schemes its' hidden corporate plans, and lobbies for political advantage, and blames the politicians when the huge corporations do not get what they want. Meanwhile, to cut their "sacred" bottom line again, the huge companies heartlessly lay-off and fire more and more, thousands and thousands of innocent, hardworking, honest Americans, that did nothing wrong, to lose their jobs, except to have the misfortune to be working for a bunch of traitorous, self-centered fools!

The politicians know they cannot very easily return fire at the big companies, since that's the group of people keeping them in office. Instead, they hurl vain insults at each other, across the party lines, and try to patch together temporary fixes. The economy is like the story of the leaking dike, and we are running out of fingers.

Do you really want to help our domestic economy? Bring home all of the overseas jobs, and make the work available to American citizens again!

Stop laying-off Americans, and lay off Chinese and Indian employees, instead. The Word of God declares that anyone that will not take care of his own household is worse than an infidel, and we are forbidden to eat with such a person. They are beneath contempt, and are stealing from their own people!

Our national leaders also need to limit such overseas activity, and not just wink at it, trying to keep their big business buddies happy. Perhaps a sort of tariff upon anything produced overseas by an American company would eliminate the greedy actions, if it costs the offenders just as much to do the factory work overseas, as to have it done, honorably, right here in the U.S.

We can also pray that the greedy hearts will be changed, and actually desire to do the correct things, and we must do that anyway. On the other hand, a few restrictive laws to motivate the large companies to think and behave more correctly will help the change along, and our domestic economy can grow strong again. I mean, really, just whose bright idea was it to actually close down U.S. Steel, in Alabama? Is there truly such a lack of vision in the leadership of our nation, that no one in authority can ever foresee a future need for our own on-board steel refinery? (A similar, but less important, thing happened about ten years ago, when they stopped making Levi blue jeans anywhere in the U.S.!)

Come on, fellow citizens, we can do better than this! Think, about the wreckage you might cause down the road, for your children, and your grandchildren. Or, is it actually possible, that your "sacred" bottom line means more to you, than the future of your own flesh and blood?

SWARMS WITH STINGERS

Abdullah of Jordan did not realize it, but a fierce battle was being fought, world-wide, over him, more than anyone else currently upon Earth. Most of the struggle was being fought in the unseen realms, where humble prayer, and faithful preaching, and exhorting, did mighty combat against lies, and deceptions, and madness, and blasphemy.

The time would soon arrive when these conflicts would be fought openly, with guns blazing, and rockets firing, and bombs blasting, and blood shedding. For now, the chess pieces were being moved around the board, as each side worked for advantage. (At any point in time, the Holy Spirit of Almighty God could easily shut down the enemy, but it seemed good in the Wisdom of God to play things out this way, instead, for the time being.)

As Abdullah fell asleep, he was once more troubled with fitful dreams, and he tossed and turned restlessly. His wife woke up, and quietly slipped out of the room, going to call the house doctor, in case Abdullah went into another seizure, or anything else. She, and all the rest of them, knew not to wake him up during the dreams, but to let them finish, and to just take care of his convulsions, by placing in a mouthpiece, so that he would not bite his own tongue, or swallow it, and also keeping him from tearing himself up in other ways, while he was "disconnected".

He began to see the nation of Pakistan, and it seemed like a high-speed time lapse film, which showed the key, and primary developments, that had produced the modern nation of Pakistan. The view was somehow a country wide span, that also showed momentary insets of zoomed in clips of certain things, as the centuries sped past.

The film had started in the distant past, right at the fall of the Tower of Babel. A certain small group of survivors had fled the destruction, escaping toward the northeast, into the mountains of what would later become large regions of India, which would later be split into Pakistan and India. The earliest cities along the Indus, instead of the Ganges, were shown to spring up and thrive, along the richly fertile Indus River Valley. The first wave ran from about 7,500 B.C., until about 4,000 B.C. Then, climate changes dried up the Indus a great amount, so that the valley could no longer support large populations, which began to drift over to the Ganges, and build new cities all up and down it.

The various warring nations all swept through the great mountainous crossroads that Pakistan had always had, and the Aryans arrived, from Eastern Europe, and Western Russia, long before anyone called them by those names. They had come with their horses to conquer and rule a warmer land than their forefathers, and the earlier Indian rulers had not yet mastered the art of either a horse cavalry, or one comprised of war-elephants. Soon, the Aryans from Europe ruled the whole Indian subcontinent, and established the caste system, and many other strange and uniquely Indian things.

Modern Pakistan sprang from those deep roots, thousands of years old, but had, in modern times, transferred its' religious fervor, as individuals, and as a culture, to the deception of Islam. Now, the Pakistani people lived entirely to destroy Israel, and the U.S. In late September, 2011, Pakistan was proven to have been guilty in the Taliban actions of attack upon the U.S. embassy in Kabul, and the assault against the foreign journalists' hotel as well, when the Pakistan intelligence service, I.S.I., helped the Taliban by giving them secret information, and weapons.

Abdullah saw a quick recent review of the power people in Pakistan, from the ruthless General Zia, to Bhutto, to Musharrev. He also saw the Taliban leaders, and the al-Queda leaders, including Bin Laden, and Zawahiri, and the rest of the Quetta Shura, the ruling council of al-Queda.

In his dream, he began to see something strange inside each one of the people he was viewing. They each seemed to have some sort of large insect trapped inside them, almost clearly visible through the person's exterior, and the insect's body aligned with the host's body, so that the heads were overlapped, and so were the arms, feet, and so on, except that the bugs had extra legs at the ribs, and also big, ugly wings, and very deadly stingers. The bugs seemed to have a long streak of thick fur running down their necks and spines, or maybe it was bug-armor, covered with fur. (Perhaps it was to shield the monsters from stinging themselves with those ultra-poisonous scorpion tails.) The bugs did not seem to be struggling to escape, or kill the hosts. Instead, they were controlling the things that the hosts said and did!

As he watched, the appearance of each one began to change further, until it seemed that the person was the one trapped on the inside of the bug, and the person actually was trying to escape, but could not. As time went on, the bug became less and less transparent, and soon, the person trapped inside became completely concealed, and struggled on vainly, screaming silently in their minds, watching their own hands and feet do things that they knew were wrong, and savage, and insane, but they had no way to stop the bugs encasing them, or kill the things from the inside. They were just dragged along for the entire horror show.

As the view zoomed out slowly, Abdullah saw millions of the huge bugs begin to take flight, and gather into massive, sky-darkening swarms, more vast than any locust plague that ever happened. They were thicker than swarms of bats leaving caves at sundown, to hunt and eat mosquitoes. They covered extensive zones of the Earth, covering whole continents, and eating away at every thing that was not already eaten up by them. The spread of them was terrifying. When zoomed in close, the view showed the individual atrocities that the monsters were wreaking, disguised within their once-human hosts. People were being murdered, raped, tortured, burned alive, rounded up into concentration camps, and systematically, ritually beheaded, because they would not worship Abdullah. (If Abdullah had ever actually read the Book of Revelation, he might have recognized those giant wasp-scorpions as a plague that was foretold, thousands of years before.)

His skin began to crawl, and his bones chilled to ice, and he began to tremble violently, the second that he heard the stone voice in his mind again. It told him that these were his advance troops, these hundreds of millions of followers, which would sting the infidels to death, since the infidels would not worship Abdullah, or the stone voice. The poison in their stings was the lying hatred they focused upon Israel, and the U.S. The stone voice told him not to be concerned about the cruel violence and bloodshed of it all, since they had to break eggs, to make omelets. The end would justify the means, just like Hitler had believed. The same lying stone graveyard voice had convinced Hitler, and it convinced Abdullah, too.

Almighty God, and His Son, King Jesus Christ, sat upon Thrones in Heaven, and listened and watched the evil vision, as the devil told it to Abdullah. After it was ended, King Jesus said to the Father,

"It's all a part of Your plan, I know, Father, but it still makes Me curious how the worm can still think it can salvage any victory at all, after Golgotha?"

The Father rumbled a hearty chuckle, smiled, and said, "Deep in its' evil heart, it knows. It is just too proud to admit the truth, even to itself!"

ONE IS THREE, THREE ARE ONE

Because of the Holy Word of God, we understand that God manifests Himself in three different roles, as He reveals Himself, to His creatures. First, as Almighty God, Creator, Father of Lights, then, second, as the Holy Son of God, King Jesus Christ, and third, as the Holy Spirit of God, indwelling all born-again followers of King Jesus Christ, and these are the three aspects and functions in which we are allowed to know Him.

Does anyone else think it more than a coincidence that in these last few years upon Earth, we are now acknowledging three widely practiced forms of water baptism? Of course, immersion is very widely used in the southern states, although there is a church at Gettysburg named "Dunker Church", where immersion was practiced, at the time of the Civil War. The church had that name because immersion was a very rare practice in those days.

Also used, worldwide, is the perhaps most ancient form of baptism, sprinkling, which originated with the Old Testament Law which specified for the High Priest to sprinkle the blood of the sacrifice upon that which was to be made Holy, unto the Lord.

The good Lord Jesus, Himself, told us to accept another form of baptism, which He specifically and personally demonstrated, when He knelt down, and washed His disciples' feet, with His Own hands, which had made the Universe. He commanded us to do likewise.

Knowing that our good Lord does not arrange things randomly, perhaps there is a correlation between the sets of threes. Is it possible that immersion corresponds to the Father? The Word says that "in Him, we live, and move, and have our being". It is impossible for anyone to escape from the Father, since all things exist within Him. He is bigger than the sky over your head, and bigger, and much more solid, than the ground under your feet!

What about foot washing? We must obviously correlate that form unto King Jesus, the Son of God, since He personally initiated it, at the Last Supper.

Then, the remaining form is sprinkling, as corresponding to the Holy Spirit. This seems quite appropriate, since the entire Old Testament was dictated by the Holy Spirit, Word by Word. Also, King Jesus clearly told us that the Holy Spirit would convict the world of sin, of righteousness, and of judgment. Jesus will not cast aside anyone who comes unto Him, but no one can come to Him, unless the Father first draws the person near, through the Holy Spirit, when the conscience of the person is triggered, with genuine guilt, and remorse, and then, confession, and repentance, follows.

Then, the person follows King Jesus,
all the Way home, to Heaven!

WEAPON OF VALOR

The American archaeologist was out in another remote location. He was climbing in hills that once had been carpeted with lush green growth, but, since certain ancient climate changes, were now mostly arid, semi-desert wilderness, in modern times. He was in a rough-terrain region, along the outer border of the Gaza Strip.

The rough, rocky land offered many natural sites that were quite useful, in which to establish little fortresses, machine-gun nests, entrenchments, and observation posts. In ancient times, the region had been much more densely populated, back when it still was very lush, and could easily support large ancient groups, and cities. It was the favorite zone for colonization by the Philistines, which were essentially adventurous Greeks, which wanted to occupy and enslave the land of Israel, and oppress the people, and steal their wealth.

While the Mycenaean Greeks were fighting the last remnants of the Minoans (the few hundred which survived the tidal wave from the eruption of Thera, named in modern times, Santorini, around 1,400 B.C.), and expanding their territory against early Etruscans, and Macedonians, and others in their neighborhood, the Philistine branch had invaded the Holy Land, and wrought all manner of death and destruction there, for a long time, from the centuries of the Judges of Israel, until King David finished killing off the very last of them, during his mighty reign. Modern Palestinians are not Philistines, at all, but are actually descendants of the Edomites, and the Amonites. They were forcibly relocated there, by Winston Churchill, to allow the Hashimites (the blood line descendants of Mohammed) to be forcibly moved into modern day Jordan.

The English wanted to give Arabia to their oil sheik buddies, instead, and they did.

As he scouted through the hills and rocks, looking for signs of ancient structures, or even pottery, he thought about the history of this place, how the modern people called themselves Philistines, but were not, and yet the ancient Philistines did once live here, thousands of years before, until King David killed them all, every last one.

He had started out early that morning, with his faithful wolf, and his faithful little gray donkey, and they had searched for hours, without finding anything of significance. For some strange reason, the man was driven to look along this side of a long, sloped ridge, which rose up to a jagged rim line of broken rock. In many places, those large boulders had come rolling on down, many of them making it all the way down the ridge, to form a jumbled curb line of rugged, huge rocks along the base.

His footing slipped a little, and he crouched into the slide, keeping his balance, barely, as he leaned uphill, until he stopped sliding, motionless, on all fours. He began to slowly work back up the few feet he had slipped, while the donkey looked at him, as if to say, "Uh huh, now you know why four legs are better than two!" The wolf barked excitedly, not helping at all, but very agitated, nonetheless.

As he stood carefully up, he noticed a little flatter place a little further along, and made toward it. Soon, they were able to perch, more reasonably horizontally, and there were a few little boulders there, which seemed stable enough to lean against, as they stopped to eat lunch, drink lots of water, and sit a moment in the shade of a very small tree there. The man closed his eyes a moment, and gave thanks, for the fine day, and his animal buddies, and the chance to explore the mysteries of ancient things, in this land of lands.

A few minutes later, he opened and blinked his eyes, in the glare, and noticed a small white thing, near the base of the tree. He crawled over carefully, to look closer, and recognized a fragment of bone, bleached white over centuries of weather exposure. A lot of the bone had eroded away, even though the zone had been arid for centuries. There was still enough rain and weather, over thousands of years, so that some wear happened.

It was not possible to tell precisely what the bone was, but it looked like it had once been a strong one, thick enough to have been used a few times as some sort of tool, maybe, by a caveman. He reached out his fingers, and carefully picked up the bone fragment.

Instantly, as with the event before, with Adam's flints, the man was suddenly in a different time, although the location was precisely unchanged. The actual perceived viewpoint was different, this time, as the man seemed not to be in his body, but just invisibly hovering, above the little ledge, about fifty feet up in the air. There were people all over the ridge wall, hundreds of them! They were all wearing crude ancient leather and metal armor, and they were all trying to get to a single person, which stood alone upon the little ledge. The man was strong, and fit looking, but did not resemble a superhero, or have bulging super-muscles. He looked like a strong, young fighter, but like many other strong, young fighters. There were one or two immediately noticeable differences, though. The young lone warrior had extraordinarily long, thick black hair, braided, and tied back down along the center of his leather sleeveless tunic. His full, long, black beard came down to the middle of his chest. Also, most young warriors fought with a sword. This man was swinging a curved, large jawbone from a donkey. He held it by the part that would form the chin, and used the jaw-hinge curve as a double-bladed cleaver of destruction, smashing and ripping through throats, skulls, chests, arms, legs, flesh, or bones, or armor, no matter what the man hit. Nothing could endure that impact. Even bronze swords were shattered like glass by the jawbone, and it was unbreakable, no matter what struck against it. The man did not seem to understand the concept of fatigue, or the simple mathematical fact that he was outnumbered, by a thousand to one. After a little while, working like a whirling helicopter blade, the man was only outnumbered by nine hundred to one.

The bodies slid down the ridge wall, piling up down below, covering completely all of the huge boulders there. The enemy soldiers tried using archers, also, but the man's arms moved even faster, and became invisible blurs, but every single arrow was both stopped, and instantly knocked straight back, like a line drive off of a bat, into the heart of the archer which shot it! After about another hundred enemy soldiers had died like that, there were no more archers left to shoot at the man. All of them had died, and slid down to join the others far below.

A couple of hundred more soldiers arrived up upon the top of the ridge, and started trying both to roll and to hurl rocks down upon the man, and also, many of them began to try scramble down the slope to reach him. Any rocks which came near, the man struck, and the rocks shattered into buckshot, which fired back at the people launching the rocks at him. Another two hundred of them died that way, plus almost a hundred more which were struck by the missiles from above, launched foolishly down upon them by their own fellow soldiers. Now, the man was outnumbered by only five hundred to one.

The battle raged on for quite a long time, and it seemed like it would never end, as the struggle entered its' ninth hour, and the shadows began to grow long across the landscape. Over nine hundred corpses were piled randomly below the man, which fought on at the same precise intensity with which he had begun the battle. The commander of the Philistines watched with an angry scowl, as more and more of his soldiers died before his eyes. Finally, when his aide told him that a thousand men had died, and asked him if he wanted to continue with the attack, the commander thought a moment, and said, "No. Call it off. He has prevailed because of the special position upon the slope, which proved unconquerable. The hills and the rocks have helped Samson live another day. We will wait, and trap him again, at a better location, which does not give him such shelter. Sound retreat!"

As Samson stood rock still, watching as every one of the living ones turned, and left, abandoning their dead, for now, he slowly relaxed, and sagged down upon a rock, and let out a long slow breath, with a shudder. As he looked up, he was suddenly overcome with critical thirst, and hoarsely cried out, "Ah, Lord God, give me a drink of water, lest I perish!"

Instantly, the jawbone in his hand, covered with human blood, became flushed with clean water, and spotlessly white, and it sprang forth a strong stream of fresh, cool, pure water. Samson drank it almost as fast as it gushed out of the jawbone. After a few minutes of that, he set the bone aside, where it continued to pour out a stream of fresh water, which he drank from several more times, letting the water soak into his flesh, and then drinking a bit more, until his thirst abated, and he completely refilled his two water-skins, and he held the jawbone over his head, and showered off the blood, and dust, and sweat of the battle, and then he stood up, placed the jawbone against the base of a very small tree, and began to carefully pick his path the rest of the way up the slope, not carrying the jawbone, but always carrying the memory of what God had just done with one solitary man, and a chunk of bone.

There would be many more battles with the Philistines, and Samson had needed to see that God would always fight inside him, and defeat all of his enemies. From this day on, Samson would never wonder again, if God would come through for him, or not.

As Samson reached the top of the ridge, climbed over, and vanished from view, the archaeologist instantly found himself back in present times, and he looked down at the bone fragment. As he opened his hand, he saw that the bone had somehow been completely crushed into powder in his clutched hand, while he was in the vision. As the wind blew the powder away, into the countryside, he wondered why the good Lord had kept the bone here for so long, but had now caused it to be destroyed.

He did not actually hear words, but the flash of understanding came immediately into his awareness, and he saw that it was kept here until he could find it, here in these final days, and then to accurately describe just how that battle of Samson's had actually happened, so that a clearer understanding could be revealed, of just how mighty and magnificent the good Lord is, and will always be, when a person will fight on His side.

The man got out his notebook, and his pen, and began to write down the most vivid elements of the vision, before the details faded. He would craft the thing into a finished written account, once he got back to his place. If the good Lord wanted it written down, accurately, and shared, immediately, then, he was not going to be the one to drag his feet about following orders!

THE BEGINNING OF THE END GAME

Abdullah of Jordan shifted restlessly in his bed, around four in the morning, and his wife awoke instantly, watching him intensely in the almost-darkness of the nightlight. She was always nervous when he began moving in his sleep, since it often meant that he was being forcibly injected with another terrifying vision from the devil. That was how he was given his marching orders, and told what and when to speak, or do, upon any major subject, and several seemingly minor ones, as well. For instance, after one rough nightmare, he started wearing only green silk ties, of a sort of sickly slime green color. His wife had asked him once about it, and he had snarled at her, "I don't know. He just said to, that's all!" She never asked again.

The dream began as they often did, with a rapid fade-in to a panoramic view, where many smaller, picture inset video clips showed here and there, within the vista, and showed some recent relevant events. In some scenes, he saw huge white wolves, hunting down and killing evil animals, before they could hurt any humans, or any innocent animals. The enormous, snow-white killers seemed to know just a few seconds before, when their intervention was needed, and they got there, with as much strength as they needed, even up to thousands of wolves, when large swarms of dangerous beasts were gathering, menacing human lands.

Time after time, the hunters found, and invisibly destroyed, the enemy animals, even including the gathering armies of sharks and sea snakes, before they could invade human habitations. They even fought against some bird flocks, since these great, mighty, supernatural wolves could also fly, as well as run, and swim.

They could not drown, or die any other way, since they had already passed through death, and had been chosen as worthy, to live again, forever.

Other scenes showed King Adam, with an armed escort of thousands of war angels, attacking and wounding many evil angels, and several evil humans, also. This group of hunter-killers kept their counterstrikes focused exclusively upon the evil men, and the evil male angels. Another scene showed Queen Eve, also escorted by thousands of lady war-angels, attacking, and killing, when needed, the evil women they found, and fighting and wounding the evil female angels they found. In other scenes, Prince Abel, the Firstborn Man of Faith, escorted by many angels, hunted down, and interfered with the evil children in the world. It was all making the devil's plans be disrupted, or canceled, or otherwise modified, so that the worm was constantly boiling over with frustrated rage, and it was not a good time to be working under his cruel claws. He always took out his rage upon his own slaves, and often, many of them were killed as a cruel result, but the devil did not care. He knew that there were plenty more, where those wretches came from. The world was an endless mother-lode of fools.

The stone voice grated like rocks grinding together in his mind, keying up every nerve in his soul to raw pain, as it ordered him to look closer, and he did, where he saw smaller scenes, but in crystal clarity, and he saw that the good angels had not only used force, directly against the ones on his side, but they could be seen whispering information to the men in the JSOC Headquarters, telling them where to find Al-Awlaki, so they could kill him with a missile strike, and where to find more al-Queda agents, the planners behind the attacks, so that the tide of battle surged to and fro, always gaining, and then falling back.

Several of the worst of the evil angels
were being bound in unbreakable chains,
and carried out to the outer darkness,
hurled there by the mighty good angels.
That was where the evil angels, at least
some of them, would remain, until called
into punishment, and thrown into the
Lake of Fire. They had already been
tried, and found guilty, when King Jesus
Christ went to the Cross, and killed sin,
forever.

Other angels were seen inside the
Pentagon, whispering thoughts into the
minds of the most brilliant and
responsive generals and admirals,
correcting a bad strategy here, or a force
misallocation there. Others were seen at
the U.N., encouraging people to forbid
Palestine to cheat its' way into
illegitimate statehood. Others were
helping to set free American hostages
from Iran, and Amanda Knox from Italy.
Others were whispering subtle advice to
big money people around the world,

helping to keep the global economy from going to meltdown, at least, not one second before it was supposed to do so. Others were reminding people to help fight human trafficking, and to fight sexual slavery, as well as poaching, and genocide. Many were on individual assignments, protecting certain individual children of light around the world, day and night. A rescue from a car wreck here, a healing from a disease there, and a million other things, were continually being done by the good angels, all of the time, everywhere, so that the evil angels were out numbered, and worn out. The enemy could not ever seem to prevail for very long, in any one place, although it did seem to do very well in Asia, Africa, Europe, and the Middle East. (Two of Putin's very finest agents, in training for a special mission two years from now, barely escaped from death upon a failed Soyuz space vessel, when they had another urgent mission come up at the last minute. It must not have yet been their time, since the good angels never missed a hit, once a contract was out on anyone, or anything.)

The ugly stone voice grated again in his thoughts, sending shockwaves of agony all up and down his spine, and making him sick in the gut. It was like an emotional hand grenade of horror, whenever the voice spoke. This time it told him that the other side had more angels, but he would soon have more people. The lies he would spin would draw in the followers, and they would stay, as willing mercenaries, once the conquering and looting began. Hundreds of millions would follow his false promises of unlimited riches, and 72 virgins, apiece, even in this present world! If a few white infidels had to lose their arrogant heads over it, well, tough. They had somehow surely stolen all of their white riches from the Arabs, anyway, or so the Arabs believed.

Besides, Pakistan was already nuclear, and was only waiting until it devised a delivery system to get a nuke all the way to the U.S., or Israel, undetected. There were a ton of volunteers, who would gladly detonate themselves with the boomer, and become vaporized in a flash of murderous stupidity.

As the dream was winding down, Abdullah's wife and the family medical staff were keeping him from biting or swallowing his tongue. They knew he would not speak to them of what he saw, or heard, but there was always some change of behavior, or strategy, right after these dreams. Sometimes, the changes were very scary. She wondered what tomorrow would reveal.

King Jesus Christ and the Father of Lights were seated upon Their thrones, watching and listening, as the dream unfolded. After it ended, King Jesus asked the Father, "Why did You let them see Our hunter-killer teams? Does that not void the element of surprise?"

The Father smiled a bit, and answered, "I have concealed them again, but for just a few minutes, I wanted the worm, and the son of perdition, the Hashimite, to see that they will not have an easy time of it. The worm is only afraid of You, My Son, but the Hashimite is only a man, that thinks he is a god, or that he should be treated like one, and he can feel fear. I wanted him to feel some genuine fear, about Us, and Our hunter-killer teams, so that he will lose much sleep, wondering when We will send them against him, personally!"

SPECIAL OPS

Four people met, and made final plans. They were standing upon the lookout balcony of the Palace of King Jesus. As they looked down upon Earth, all four of them, including King Jesus (the Holy Son of God), and Michael (the Green Cherub of Space), and Gabriel (the Red Cherub of Time), and Tzedek-el (the High General of the War Angels of Heaven), noticed different features and points of interest in the aspects of the things which they observed. King Jesus saw all of the aspects and points, and drew focus upon the most essential details, so that all of them would understand their own particular part in the op.

Then, after all was settled, King Jesus, looking at Tzedek-el, and laying a friendly hand upon the angel's shoulder, said, "All right, My old friend. I know that you will not fail in your mission.

Remember how you killed all of the Syrian army one night, all by yourself? This mission will be easier, even with steel armor involved, since you are allowed to use any and all force, even, if you deem it necessary, the equivalent of a tactical nuke. Just try to keep the radiation levels down, since I will want to rebuild it later, during the Thousand Years. Now, you are blessed in the Name of the Father, the Savior, and the Holy Spirit! I will be watching, and both of these mighty war-cherubs will also fight, helping you. Now, go!"

As the King finished, all three of the others leapt into the air, streaking outward in a tight group, and vanishing behind the moon, hidden from Earth's prying eyes. The telescopes of men would never see them, but the evil angels could, so the good Lord had rendered the moon opaque to the eyes of the evil angels, so it could be used as a launching spot. The two cherubs and the angel watched right through the moon, anyway, since the Lord had left their eyes un-held, and they waited until the precise moment that the moon, the Space Station, and the target entry window all lined up. In a flash, all three of them streaked instantly and invisibly straight through the 2,000 miles of the moon, and shot out the near side, speeding like gigantic laser beams past the Space Station, where they suddenly split, with the two cherubs driving like arrows into the devil, where he was "hiding", in Quetta, Pakistan. They let him see them at the last possible split second, way too late for him to block or dodge the impact, but just long enough for him to feel absolute shock, which froze him in place a split second longer, so that they hit him at the same precise moment, full strength and force! It was like being hammered by two small planets, moving at about light speed. Nothing but a thing that used to be a cherub could have even survived the collision. (The good cherubs had been equipped with a special blessing from King Jesus, and that was collision-proof.)

The worm screamed in pain and terror, feeling that his wings and legs had been completely torn off! He tried to mouth curses at the cherubs, which had once been his peers, but his jaws were broken, and all that came out was some vile spittle, and strangling noises. The so-called "dragon" was having a hard time, just trying to breathe. The agony was beyond human comprehension.

The two cherubs walked back over to where the worm had landed, and looked down silently. The pure contempt and hatred was not upon the devil's face, but upon the faces of the good cherubs. The worm had been one of them, their friend, and he had betrayed and deceived all of them, and had then also killed their two most favorite friends, Adam and Eve. They knew that it was okay to hate him forever. The worm was not ever going to be forgiven, so they did not have to forgive him.

The dragon looked up at them, and then, he spit out broken fangs, and blood, and said, painfully, "Just finish it!" The thing's face had been terribly deformed by evil, and was never again to be the beautiful eagle-faced aspect of the Golden Cherub of Matter, since the dragon would never again be a cherub.

The lion-faced Green Cherub of Space and the man-faced Red Cherub of Time looked at each other, and then back at the worm, and then they began to laugh: a deep, hearty, happy sound. Gabriel said, "Now, you know we won't do that. Only the Lord will kill you, in the Lake of Fire, when the time has come. In the meantime, even though your wings and legs are already beginning to grow back, and heal, this will keep you out of our way, for long enough."

With his last word, Gabriel and Michael both launched back up toward

Heaven, having done their parts of the op successfully. As they vanished, upward, the enemy shouted, "Wait! Long enough for WHAT?!"

The only answer he heard was their fading laughter.

Meanwhile, Tzedek-el had flown undetected, and unopposed, all the way deep into North Korea. The second he arrived, at his first target zone, he leveled a concealed nuke weapons lab, and left it and everyone working there in a smoldering, glowing crater. His next stop was a nearby set of underground silos. They were well concealed, and hardened, but not war-angel proof. He left more smoldering craters. Then he made it to a set of "hidden" tunnels, crammed full of tanks, missiles, aircraft, supplies, and over a hundred thousand North Korean troops, buried deep underground. They would remain buried underground, from now on.

From there, it was on to destroy a communications center in the capital, and to cave in some special deep hardened bunkers, where the big shots would have hidden. After that, he streaked down to the coastline, and sank every North Korean submarine. (They did not have any? Oh yes, they did, too, thanks to their Chinese buddies!) Over a dozen special small subs were scuttled that night. The final step of the mission was almost ready. A grand total of 46 seconds had elapsed, since the war-angel's first move.

Suddenly, a demon charged toward Tzedek-el, which made him roar with joy! The fight was extremely intense, and lasted only about four seconds, although the two combatants were moving in an invisible blur, at such a high rate of speed, that the equivalent would have been like humans fighting for over a month, without stopping!

This fight was the last stage of the angel's mission. The two cherubs had blocked out the dragon, and Tzedek-el had destroyed all of the North Koreans' massing forces, to stop a secret attack that was planned soon, to invade and conquer South Korea. The second purpose of the angel's attack had been to draw out this particular demon, which was one of the tougher ones, and to make him lose control of his temper, so that Tzedek-el could lock him into combat.

Tzedek-el was the General of the War Angels of Heaven, and he had never lost a fight, or failed a mission, and he never would. That deadly killer angel loved King Jesus Christ more than his own life, and he would never lose a fight for his King, no matter what!

After he had beaten and subdued the demon, he wrapped him in golden, unbreakable chains of truth, and dragged him out to the edge of the universe. The good angel stopped, with his mighty arm drawn back, and asked, "Well Lord, do

You still want this thing thrown out, into the Void?"

Tzedek-el clearly heard the Voice of his Master in his mind. King Jesus answered him, "Yes. Otherwise, he will only stir up more trouble, somewhere else. He can stay in chains, out there in the dark and cold, and wait a few years, while he thinks about what he did, and waits for the Lake of Fire!"

MESSIAH, MESSAGE, MEDIA, MEN

Some of us are old enough to remember the Sixties, and to remember them as an actual set of memories and experiences. For anyone too young for that, news films, newspapers, and the "good old days" stories from the Baby Boomers will have to paint the picture more fully for you.

Paint is actually a good place to start. Before the Sixties, paint was something to keep metal from rusting, and wood from rotting. During the Sixties, artists like Andy Warhol, Peter Max, and many, many others proved to the whole world that paint was capable of impacting the way that people thought, felt, and acted. Warships were still painted gray, and combat uniforms were still camouflage, but every other object and surface was up for grabs. Open season was declared, to experiment with any and all extreme visual effects.

Audio experiences were launching into unexplored territory, also, with the most creative era in music, especially Rock and Roll. New technologies were helping the widespread propagation of strange, never-before-seen-or-heard things, and the governments of the world played around with mind control, propaganda, and world-wide publicity stunts. The West was well aware of the impact that Sputnik had made in the minds and attitudes of the people of the world. It mattered what pictures and sounds made it out to the rest of the world, no matter if the interested parties were governments, corporations, or individuals.

Braniff Airlines painted their planes a new wild pattern, and their "stewardesses" all wore new, colorful, modern art outfits. Everything was sort of going psychedelic, and "far-out, man". Bell bottom jeans, platform shoes (for guys and gals, alike), longer hair, tie-dyed t-shirts, beads, flowers, leather clothes, denim everything, VW busses, and FM stereo radio stations were just natural developments, in a culture that now knew just how powerful bright colors, and loud, strange sounds, could become.

Minds could be manipulated, and hearts could be turned. Crooked advertising people tried using subliminal ads, until the F.C.C. made them all stop it. Social researchers have well proven that the fall of the Iron Curtain, and the Berlin Wall, was achieved more by the music of the Beatles, than by the out-spend-and-collapse-them-into-poverty strategy that was applied by Ronald Reagan and William Casey. Change the thoughts, and then you can change the results.

Some of the people living way back then, with me, in ancient times, noticed many correlations between the means by which a message was delivered, and the impact of the message upon the target audience. A man named Marshall McLuhan wrote a book called "Understanding Media", in which he details how various information delivery systems affect, by their very nature, how well or poorly the message can be received.

A rough example might be that a television will not reach a man without sight, especially if the sound is muted. A radio cannot deliver a message to a deaf man. The U.N. understands this concept, or they would not employ hundreds of full-time translators. Information cannot be communicated, unless it is presented in a form that the intended target can understand. This affects the choices made, therefore, by every person trying to transfer information from a source to a target. Even if the info hits the target, it has to be the right ammo, sent the right way, or the mission fails.

This reminds one of the old joke where scientists said that they had perfected the D.N.A. for making a politician that could not tell a lie, but that they never could get him elected! It does seem that a lot of people would rather elect a comfortable lie, instead of a troubling truth. No one ever won an election by honestly telling the people a thing that they needed to hear, but that they did not want to accept. Honest politicians, if they get elected at all, seldom see a second term.

Those of us trying to live out the role of a truthful Christian witness, to the truthfulness of the Word of God, and the faithfulness of God, and the power of the Holy Spirit, are constantly being hit with cheap shots, often from people that themselves claim to be Christians, but do not act anything like it. Anytime some little creep spots a microscopic imperfection in the faithful Christian, the scumbag will crow out loud about it, trying to humiliate the slightly imperfect

Christian. When the other person should offer encouragement, to walk out the faith, in a better Way, the hypocrite instead verbally slaps another human that stumbled, because the hypocrite has a heart without love. The false-hearted hypocrite knows deep inside that he is a loser, and a failure as a Christian, so he desperately hunts to hurt better Christians, to try to drag everyone else down to his own sewer level of sin.

The most important message ever sent is that Jesus Christ is the Holy Son of God, and that He saves us from our sin. King Jesus answered the Jews (that demanded a sign from Him) that they would never believe unless they saw signs and wonders, but no sign would be given unto them, except the sign of the prophet Jonah. Jesus would be in the Earth for three days, and three nights, just like Jonah had been, and then, He would also return.

The number one, most important component, of the message was the identity of King Jesus Christ, and that He was actually God, in the flesh. If people did not accept that fact, they could not be saved, not if they thought that He was a liar. He said Himself that the ones that rejected Him would have no excuse, because He had worked among them miracles and signs which no on else had ever done, in the whole history of the Earth.

His greatest miracles were the execution of all evil, forever, by paying for all sin, for all men, with His Own Life, and then, three days later, taking up His Own Life once again, as the Father had given Him commandment to do.

He is still working miracles every day and night, since every person that is ever saved is saved by King Jesus, and no one else! The grand miracle of His Resurrection was the final evidence that even skeptics could not deny, even though they still try, just so they will not have to try to obey King Jesus Christ. The good Lord will still have His Way, in the long run. That's fine, with those of us which love Him!

King Jesus said that for this cause He was brought forth, that He might bear witness to the truth. The truth is that God is real, and alive, and He really is God, and He really is good! King Jesus also revealed to us that no man has seen God at any time, but the Only Begotten Son of God has fully shown God unto us, since the Son is also God!

There could be no more fitting and perfectly selected Messenger, to deliver the most important message. Jesus Christ is the Message, and Jesus Christ is the Messenger, too.

The truth is that God is powerful, and truthful. King Jesus Christ proved His divine power by His miracles. He proved His divine truthfulness by His Own Resurrection!

Media and Message were the same: Yeshua Messiah!

THE CURSE OF PHARAOH

"And another Pharaoh arose, who knew not Joseph..."

Abdullah of Jordan began another dream. He saw the head of the Iranian special ops branch set in place an assassination plot, with twin prongs. One target of the hit squad was the Arabian Ambassador to the U.S., and the other target was the Israeli Ambassador to the U.S., but the plots were uncovered, and thwarted. He saw the Egyptians using brutal force against Egyptian Christians, even crushing many of them under armored vehicles, and firing live ammo into crowds of peaceful protestors. Egypt had been stirring up trouble against everyone in sight, including Israel, the U.S., and even themselves, as the people protested against the military, for not having moved, at all, toward forming a real, lawful, civilian government. The uproar had hurt the tourist industry, so times were harder.

Even Muslim Egyptians and Christian Egyptians were at each others' throats, with the Muslims burning down a Christian church, which had triggered the Christian protests, which had then triggered the murderous response by the Egyptian "government" (military). At least 25 were killed, and hundreds more were seriously injured.

He saw Syrian agents in the U.S. video-recording and spying upon Syrian protestors in the U.S., so that retribution could be dealt unto their families back home in Syria. Some people were killed in Syria, because of what their kinfolks protested, half a world away!

Even with all of the victories for the dark side, there were also some victories for light. Five nuclear scientists in Iran were somehow mysteriously hunted down and executed. It would not stop the

Iranian nuclear program, but it would slow it down, some. Earthquakes hit Pakistan again, destroying a secret weapons' supply road through the mountains, which had been a pipeline for bombs, for the Taliban and al-Queda to use, in Afghanistan, and anywhere else they wanted.

The Chinese had been attempting to strengthen their buddies, the North Koreans, for a long time, and had spent much money and effort upgrading the North Korean military, trying to prepare them to become powerful combat allies, in coming military campaigns in Asia. All of that went up in smoke, after the General, Tzedek-el, had finished his strike mission against several "secret" military assets that the Chinese and the North Koreans had been building up, for the last 15 years. (Because the embarrassment would be unthinkable, and the string of defeats unexplainable, both the North Koreans, and the Chinese, had kept their lips shut about the damage that one war-angel had wrought, in less than a minute.) It gave them all nightmares from that point forward, while they agonized about what strange new secret strike weapon the West had just applied against them. They did not believe in angels, or demons, but they did believe in weapons.

As his fitful dream continued, Abdullah heard the scary stone voice whisper that the battle was not going smoothly, and he had better start to get his own Jordanian military in better shape, and to keep in closer touch with his allies, which would ultimately become his followers, in the next few years. It was time to get the ball rolling. He was instructed to reel in Ahmadinajab, and keep him from starting trouble among the allies, or trying to set them against each other. Otherwise, the Iranian would be removed, painfully.

While Abdullah continued dreaming, in Amman, Tzedek-el, and some of his other war-angels, hovered over the border between Israel and Egypt. Another separate band of them was miles away, hovering over the northern border, guarding Israel, and watching toward Syria. The General had some of his closest and toughest friends at both locations. They were some of the ones which had first helped him and the good cherubs battle against the enemy and its' angels, in the First War. They spoke mind-to-mind, even miles apart.

Tzedek-el said, "Well, Egypt has always been a particular problem for Hebrews, all of the way back to Hagar, Abraham's concubine, and from her came Ishmael, who is the father of a world full of troublemakers. The worst of the trouble, in ancient times, was the time after Joseph, until Moses. The Egyptians were exceedingly cruel, and terrifyingly brutal. They held their place in history by savagery, and by sheer, raw force. In modern times, Egypt is the beginning of the terrorist movement, and the start of the horrible concept of Shariah law, which is the least tolerant, and very most vicious and brutal of all types of Muslim styles. Zawahiri is an Egyptian, and one of the worst enemies of our good Lord."

"Many nations have tried to destroy the Hebrews, ever since the times of the Patriarchs, in their beginning, in Hebron. Even though they were scattered, worldwide, they were never annihilated, completely. 'The People of the Book', as they call themselves, still were kept alive upon the Earth, by our good Lord, King Jesus Christ. Now, they are being gathered home again, to Israel."

"As the gathering of Hebrews thickens, intensely, so will the enemy's efforts to overcome them. We must, from now on, stay very nearby, on location at the borders. No incursions will be tolerated. Use whatever force you deem needed, short of nuclear. Never forget what Egypt did (and tried to do worse) unto the

Hebrews, centuries ago, and God broke Egypt from a world-power to a nothing minor player, ever since. Still, they refused to learn, and the curse of their ancestors is still upon them, at least upon the individuals which would not repent. If they continue to try to attack Israel, or even the Egyptian Christians, start taking out the individual aggressors, and keep things quiet, until we receive further orders!"

The General, and all of the others there, over a thousand strong, at both locations, became silent, staring down at the territory below, scanning everything, and everyone, with the kind of sight that only angels have, seeing in every wavelength of the entire electromagnetic spectrum. Visible light, x-rays, gamma rays, and cosmic rays were all open to the supernatural sight which the angels possessed, as well as infrared, and all of it. They also could perceive the spirits, and nothing could hide from them. Israel slept soundly that night, as it had, many thousands of nights before, with the wings of the war-angels of God stretched wide over them.

THE NEXT TIME I MET GWEN

A third of a century is a long time. A lot of changes can, and do, happen in that much time.

Time's march had left some scars and bruises upon each of us, but I still saw and heard the same sweet girl I once knew, decades before. There was some more gray, in our hair, and a few little crows' feet, at the corners of our eyes, and a few more laugh lines, and yet, by far, the greatest of the facial changes had happened to me, with many more scars, and the addition of a trim beard, now turned gray, with still some brown and gold mixed in (just to remind me that I used to be young!) She told me that I was very slim. I answered that it had taken a lot of exercise, and careful food choices, to try to maintain things like that. She still looked very pretty, but I knew neither one of us was likely to want to go for a 3-mile run later, like we used to do often.

Both of us were still strong, and active, and living out busy lives, working to live productively, and peacefully. I still do not know why she looked me up, after almost 33 years, of absolute silence, but it was a stunner, when I heard her voice on the message machine, one afternoon. I called her back, then we talked for hours, and a friendship long ago abandoned for dead was re-awakened.

Her adventures had included a marriage, four children, many horses, and cows, and chickens, and such, and a fascinating career with Lockheed, as the design crew chief for the starboard side wiring, for the F-16 fighter. She had become expert at computer design, and real-world applications, including having to crawl up inside the F-16 model at Lockheed, to actually tape-measure the precise length for particular wiring assemblies. (The starboard side is entirely different from the port side, which had its' own design crew, just like hers'.)

There were many fascinating events and evolutions that she revealed, and I also shared all of mine. She was pleased, and surprised, to find out that I have become a writer, and, she later read, and liked, my books, and encouraged me with certain faith that they will sell very well, given time. I have that same hope, or I would not have worked so hard to keep writing them.

Unfortunately, not all of the changes were happy ones, and the most painful one for her was her divorce. Sometimes, couples stay together, sometimes, not. Sometimes, separations are reasonable, sometimes, not. Sometimes, even the children can be caught up in the struggle, and used like playing pieces upon a chessboard. No one wins, in cases like that, especially the children. (Well, maybe the attorneys all win, because of their fees.)

Not all of my own changes were so great, either. I will not recount my troubles here, but, I did have a share of them. If the good Lord had not gotten each of us through our difficulties, I am certain that we would not have survived.

The part of our reunion, which was the finest, for me, was that Gwen now had a deeper love and respect for the things of our good Lord, and prayed often, and read her Bible, and listened to Christian music, in her car, and now was genuinely saying "thank you" for every kindness, courtesy, or gift, and meaning it. The joy in her spirit was a thing of greatly increased beauty, despite the hard things her heart had suffered. The Lord had stayed with her, and brought her through things, and made her grow stronger, tougher, and more humbly thankful. (What a God, what a woman, and what a miracle all of that was!)

I could see evidence of some similar changes in myself, and I also remembered that they had been anything but pleasant, at the time that I was being carved into something new. I guess sometimes the good Lord uses the very hardest of things to re-shape our minds and hearts, and to focus our awareness more fully, upon Himself. I do not think that hard times always mean that God is angry with you, or that you did something wrong, or even that you need to be corrected. Sometimes, I guess it is more a matter of being "forged", as in a hot fire. I do not guess that the steel enjoys the process much more than we do.

So, even though the romance died off, long decades ago, and we each went our separate ways, on into our own futures, our good Lord was still watching over each of us. Now, our friendship is re-awakened, but, even more importantly, our brother-and-sister relationship in

King Jesus Christ is renewed, and much richer, and stronger than ever. With, or without any romance, we will still travel into the future together, as will all of the other children of Light, with us. Also, now another fan has joined my growing number of readers, and is also encouraging me to keep writing.

She agreed with many other friends of mine who have said that I did, indeed, meet my main two goals in writing these books: 1. that our good Lord will be glorified, and 2. that the reader does enjoy the books, and will maybe even recommend them to a friend. I hope so.

I know that my friends are kind-hearted, or else they would not be my friends for long. Still, I think Gwen would tell me, if she thought the books were not fine. She tends to be simply straight with people, about her opinion, with diplomacy, if possible. (She would not spare my feelings, even if she was my girlfriend for a couple of years, long ago.)

It was good to see her again, like a 33-year college reunion, but more personal. It was good to find peace, about old times and things, and to focus upon new hopes for the future. Our Lord is merciful.

IN, FOR THE DURATION

(NOTE: We are commanded, by King Jesus, to "speak the truth, in love". Know that such is precisely what this chapter is all about. This is, to the very best of my understanding, the correct truth. It is also written in the sincerest motive of genuine brotherly love, since I want all of our brothers and sisters to understand the truth, including me. Agree, or do not, just only let your curiosity become provoked, but not your anger, please!)

My Dad was a real, honest-to-goodness war hero, from WWII. Even in an era when nearly every man was a hard-nosed warrior, a tough guy, and a two-fisted citizen soldier, my Dad, and many others like him, stood as excellent, brave, steel-hearted leaders, which looked death right in the face, and tried to shoot it right between the eyes, first! A frequently heard saying around here was "Hit him again, harder!" WWII men knew how to take care of business.

Dad told me fascinating stories of his time as a P.T. boat skipper, streaking across choppy waves in the dark, to chase down and torpedo enemy ship after enemy ship. They had a ship's compass on the bridge which used ultra violet light to illuminate the markings upon the compass and needle, since the P.T. boats ran completely dark, without even running lights, when they were hunting. His watch and pocket compass also came with phosphorescent markings. Even in the absolute dark, they still had to know where they were headed, and what time it was, so that they got there on time. (It's the same thing for us, in this dark world of these Last Days.)

Dad had a gift for strategy, and he never lost a battle, so they kept promoting him. For the last two years of the war, he was the Executive Officer of the P.T. Task Force, which was based upon the Philippine Island of Leyte. This included about 150 P.T. boats, and their total support needs and maintenance workers. He was the second-in-command only to the Commanding Officer. (If J.F.K. had still been skipper of his own sunken P.T. boat, he would have been taking orders from my Dad. Instead, J.F.K. was already back stateside.)

One time I asked Dad if he ever got tired of being in the war, and wanted to come home. He laughed, and said, "Sure! However, we all knew that we were 'in, for the duration.'"

Since I was only about 11 or 12, I asked him to explain that term. He said that it meant that nobody went home, until the war was either won, or lost. There would be no "early outs". "In, for the duration."

My parents' marriage was also like that, in terms of permanent commitment. They only married once, to each other, and neither one would ever want anyone else. Dad proved that, when he stayed here after Mom had graduated to Heaven, for another 5 and 1/2 years. He went out square-dancing, as many as five nights a week, but he never wanted to marry anyone after Mom. She was the love of his life, even after she was gone. She felt the same way about him.

I think that our modern society, with all of its' high speed everything, instant everything else, and drive-through existence, has jaded our sense of perspective about long-term commitment, and faithful, permanent loyalty, even under hard duress. People today have conditioned themselves to look for quick, easy answers, to everything, and life is just not, in actual reality, structured to operate like that. People seem more interested in covering up and numbing out the symptoms, instead of properly diagnosing, and then curing the root of the problem. We need to think more in

terms of permanence, not quick-fixes.
Quick-fixes usually do not last very long.

King Jesus Christ told us a parable
about the Word of God, as seed, and
people who heard the Word as various
types of soil. Some fell by the wayside,
and birds (evil spirits) came and
devoured it, so that the people could not
believe, and thus be saved. Some was
upon rocky soil, without much earth,
where it sprang up quickly, but withered
when the sun arose and scorched it,
because it had no depth of earth. These
folks, He said, were those who
immediately received the Word with
gladness, but, later, when temptation, or
tribulation, or persecution, came, because
of the Word, these also failed, because
they had no depth of commitment to
Him.

If the first century Christians had had
no depth of commitment unto our good
Lord, we likely would not have ever
heard of Him. They had to hang tough,

all the Way through it, and trust the good Lord to bring them each home safely, after the war. He did, because they did. He brought them through it, because He knew that they would try to obey Him, and to endure whatever He needed them to endure. He knew that they really were "in, for the duration".

Is there really anyone still out there that does not yet realize that we have entered the very Last Days of the world? We truly are the Last Days' Christians, and, according to Bible Prophecy, we are in store for a very rough time. Please, do not blindly accept any well-meaning (but mistaken) person's vain hope, that we are not going to have to fight through, and be slaughtered during, the Great Tribulation.

Learn basic self-defense, and learn basic weapon's training. If you, the Men of the House, will not do it for yourselves, please, please do it for your wives and children, since they will have to rely upon you for their literal survival!

Do not count upon the police, when order breaks down. They will already be overloaded, or else, order could not break down.

Do I scare you? Good! Probably not near enough! This is not a joke, and this is NOT a drill!

Okay, okay, I know, you are likely saying, "Well, people have been saying that sort of thing for centuries, and it never has happened." True. So far. Just because a thing has never happened before, in all of history, does that mean that it cannot ever happen? Choose what you want to believe, live your own life, but never say that you were not warned. That's what I am doing, right now: warning you!

I have become completely convinced, by Prophecy, dreams, and the daily news, that we have crossed the threshold into the final seven years. What if I'm right about that? Well, it means that we have no "pre-tribulation-rapture" event to hope for. Otherwise, why are we all still here? Could it happen that all Christians, everywhere, passed over the seven year mark, and were all "left behind"? That does indeed seem to agree with Scripture, but the "pre-tribulation-rapture" concept does not seem to be validated by the red-ink Words of King Jesus Christ, although some of my closest brothers and sisters in Christ still favor that notion. I am not writing this material to offend anyone, but to shine more light into some dark corners, of confusion, so that we can really see whatever's really there. I therefore suggest a "follow the evidence" type of approach to this issue, since that is a proven scientific method of investigation, and also works effectively in matters of law.

First, we need to agree upon a source of authority, for a solid foundation of precise and correct information. I nominate the Holy Son of God, since He is the Living Truth, and He knows all things. Agreed?

All right. The red-ink Words of King Jesus will be the prime reference for this research. Any other Scriptures, except what is recorded as direct quotes, from the Holy Son of God, will be discounted as secondary in value, whether contained in a letter by Paul, or Peter, or anyone else.

Beginning in Matthew, we can see a number of Prophecies by King Jesus, Himself, about the nature and manner of His Own return, and the sequence of events which He will unfold, when the time is right. (Get out your Bibles, since you may not trust me to have interpreted the Word of God correctly, but please, remember that the N.I.V. is not the literal Word of God. It is a paraphrase, and is not literal. Either King James, or New King James, will do fine. If you do not have those, use whatever version that you have handy.)

Now, I will list some of the references that I was given the grace to spot, and, if you will proceed with a flexible, open mind, and a humble heart, I will try to share with you what has been shown unto me.

MATTHEW:
1. Ch. 13: 24-30
2. Ch. 13: 37-43
3. Ch. 13: 47-50
4. Ch. 24: 13
5. Ch. 24: 20-24
6. Ch. 24: 26-27
7. Ch. 24: 29-31
8. Ch. 24: 42
9. Ch. 25: 31-33

MARK:
1. Ch. 13: 5
2. Ch. 13: 10
3. Ch. 13: 14
4. Ch. 13:18-27
5. Ch. 13: 29-33

LUKE:
   1. Ch. 9: 26
   2. Ch. 11: 29-32
   3. Ch. 11: 49-51
   4. Ch. 12: 36-40
   5. Ch. 12: 42-46
   6. Ch. 13: 24-30
   7. Ch. 17: 22-37
   8. Ch. 21: 24-36

JOHN:
   1. Ch. 17: 15

REVELATION:
   1. Ch. 6: 9-13
   2. Ch. 7: 13-14
   3. Ch. 12: 10-11
   4. Ch. 12: 17
   5. Ch. 13: 5-7
   6. Ch. 14: 12-16

The references in Revelation still do qualify as direct quotes from King Jesus

Christ, since it is the transcription of a direct mind-to-mind vision, in perfect clarity, which Jesus imparted into John.

Now, please actually look all 29 of them up, and read them for yourself, in a literal version, and pray for the good Lord to open up your perception, even further, to clearly comprehend the accurate truth about these matters. Set aside your long-held traditions, and your pre-conceptions, and let the Word of God and the Holy Spirit direct your viewpoint in these things. Agree with the good Lord, even if you do not agree with me. I am convinced that His Own Words will always be the most accurate source of truth and understanding.

May our good Lord always bless you, Brother, or Sister, as you pursue your own continued research into His Word, and continue to walk in His Way!

ABOUT THE AUTHOR

The main thing that I try to do is to accurately transcribe the dreams and visions, which have been arriving in a steady stream, ever since I was very little. I do not hear voices, except as part of a dream, as in dialogue, but I do see vivid, intense pictures, somewhere upon that internal video screen that we all have. I think maybe the good Lord wants me to share them with all of our brothers and sisters, since they are the richest treasures which I have to share.

I do not know, yet, if there will be a seventh book, or not. Between staying up late most nights, finishing a story, and being awakened very often during the night anyway, by vivid, intense, full-color, 3D, stereo-surround (and usually dramatic, as well) type dreams, I find myself in a bit of fatigue.

Perhaps a brief rest, then whatever the good Lord wants me to do, after that. I hope that you like the books.

And I looked, and behold a white cloud, and upon the cloud One sat like unto the Son of Man, having on His head a golden crown, and in His hand a sharp sickle.

And another angel came out of the Temple, crying with a loud voice to Him that sat on the cloud, "Thrust in Thy sickle, and reap: for the time is come for Thee to reap; for the harvest of the Earth is ripe."

And He that sat on the cloud thrust in His sickle on the Earth; and the Earth was reaped.

Revelation 14: 14-16, KJV

HARVEST MOON